I0601252

CLEO BROWNE

DRMC – Devil's Rose Merry Christmas

First published by Meihana PinkerLtd 2024

Copyright © 2024 by Cleo Browne

All rights reserved. No part of this publication may be reproduced, stored or transmitted in any form or by any means, electronic, mechanical, photocopying, recording, scanning, or otherwise without written permission from the publisher. It is illegal to copy this book, post it to a website, or distribute it by any other means without permission.

This novel is entirely a work of fiction. The names, characters and incidents portrayed in it are the work of the author's imagination. Any resemblance to actual persons, living or dead, events or localities is entirely coincidental.

Cleo Browne asserts the moral right to be identified as the author of this work.

Cleo Browne has no responsibility for the persistence or accuracy of URLs for external or third-party Internet Websites referred to in this publication and does not guarantee that any content on such Websites is, or will remain, accurate or appropriate.

Designations used by companies to distinguish their products are often claimed as trademarks. All brand names and product names used in this book and on its cover are trade names, service marks, trademarks and registered trademarks of their respective owners. The publishers and the book are not associated with any product or vendor mentioned in this book. None of the companies referenced within the book have endorsed the book.

First edition

This book was professionally typeset on Reedsy.
Find out more at reedsy.com

Contents

To my readers

To my lovely readers, phew, what a year it's been!
I started this whole author thing as an experiment to see whether or not I could even write a book. Then I uploaded it to Amazon as another experiment to see if anyone other than friends and family would read it and wow!
The support I've gotten from you, the readers, has been mind-blowing.
Thank you, for taking the time to read my books, send me messages, or engage with me on social media. I truly, truly appreciate you all.
This Christmas novella is dedicated to you all.

Merry Christmas from me and the DRMC family.

Chapter 1

Marx

"What the fuck are they doing?" I mutter under my breath. With Christmas a week away and a lot on our plates I figured Church first thing would mean I'd get them ready for business.

Instead, I've got almost a dozen men standing around Jovie's tablet, watching something intently, and then trying to emulate what's on the screen.

"It's to the left, you dick! If you don't get it right Jovie's Tiktok will be ruined!" Rider growls. I don't know who he's talking to, seeing as all of them moved the same way, except him.

I figure I should stop this shit now, otherwise we'll never get anything done. "Church! Prospects, you too," I stomp to my place at the head of the table and sit down heavily.

Christmas is always a busy fucking time, especially when the club owns so many businesses and I'm the mug who does the bulk of the paperwork. My men file in, all in high spirits from their early morning fuck around or from the project we've been working on. A month back Tav suggested that our last run before the weather got too cold should be a toy run. It was a huge success and for the past two weeks the Ol Ladies have been wrapping them for the MC to deliver to the families we know will be struggling this time of year. Mama Debs even made a shit ton of frozen Christmas meals for them to enjoy too, taking the pressure off some already stressed moms and dads. Everyone takes their places, my officers either side of me, the rest of the brothers in their usual seats. Because the prospects aren't usually in here they've stationed themselves against the wall.

"Is there a reason Chomper is in Church?" Dex asks, pointing to the gator nestled in the baby carrier Rhodie is wearing.

"Yeah, Chewy was meeting a client this morning, and her brothers," Rhodie gives Tav a pointed look, "Wouldn't look after their nephew,"

"I'm not sure a gator counts as a nephew," Tav replies drily.

"Shhh! You'll make him feel bad!" Rhodie says, covering what he thinks are Chomper's ears.

"Dude, how do you know that's where his ears are?" Nitro asks my brother.

"I dunno. I figured they were on the side of his head like everyone else's," Rhodie shrugs.

"Wire, you're the only person allowed a device in here, Google where Chomper's ears are."

"Fucks sake!" I interrupt, "Gator ears are near the top of their heads, that flap part behind their eyes." They all fall silent and stare at me as I pinch the bridge of my nose and take deep breaths like Gus taught me. Although, come to think of it, Gus isn't all that chill so maybe this shit doesn't work.

"Pres is right, Chomper's ears are that flap behind his eyes," Wire corroborates.

"Thank you, Wire. Now can we get on with this shit?" A

dozen heads all nod, and I don't miss the smirks on the ex Death Rider's faces. They love this shit. "Anyway, I know it's early morning and we don't usually meet at this time, so I'll make it a quick one. I just want updates on how our Christmas project is running."

Tank, my secretary clears this throat. "We've delivered food and toy packages to 67 families so far."

"Good work, brothers." I bang my palm on the table a few times to show my appreciation.

Tank continues, "There's still roughly 100 more deliveries to do. The Ol Ladies are wrapping the final presents and Takoda and Debs are working on the last meals to be packaged and go out. We'll be done with the deliveries by tomorrow night I'd say."

"On that note, has anyone seen the invoice for the groceries? It hasn't come across my desk yet." I look around at my brothers before noticing that Tav has his hand up.

"I'm sorry if we stepped on any toes, but Tombs Security donated the food for the Christmas packages." He says nervously.

"Thank Tombs Security on our behalf, Tav." I say, tipping my chin in gratitude. "Well, DRMC, by tomorrow night there will be 167 families with presents and full bellies for Christmas."

The brothers all look very pleased with themselves. It's been a mammoth task, but we've all pulled together. This is the first time we've done something like this, and I think this is something we'll put in our calendar to do every year. Everyone needs a little Christmas cheer, and if we can lean into poker runs or other fundraisers to get this done, then so be it.

"Right, I'm proud of you boys, and I'm especially proud of our women who have put a lot of fucking effort into this. Because of that, I want to make their first DRMC Christmas special for them and the kids. More memorable than watching Uncle Rider get wasted in an elf costume. Like he does every year." Rider crosses his arms and glares at me, while the rest of the brothers snicker.

"You fuckers love it! I bring Christmas cheer!" Rider grumbles.

"Alright then, Mr Christmas Cheer, what do you suggest we do to make this year special for our family?" Fox says, eyebrows raised at my SAA.

"Well, we'll need a fucking tree for starters." He glares.

"Nat mentioned putting up lights, so we can do that," Savage offers.

"I think that we should probably do some gift shopping too," Judge offers, but I don't miss the grimace on his face before he perks up, "That can be one of your jobs, prospects."

The look of horror on the prospects faces is fucking delightful.

"Right, you know what to do. Organize yourself into groups and get shit done. I'm sure the women will be more than happy to tell you where to put the decorations." I chuckle as I bring the gavel down, trusting my men to figure this shit out for themselves. Realizing what I've asked of them, I yell "Church in two days to report back on progress!" I trust my men with my life, but this? This is something that could get out of hand without proper supervision. I'll ask Mama Debs to oversee them, just in case.

They filter out of church, some looking thoughtful, some like Rider looking fucking giddy at the thought of tormenting the prospects with his unreasonable gift ideas. I know that man well enough that there are going to be some awful gifts being given. He's like a fucking kid.

"Tav! Hold back a moment," Tav hovers by the door. For a

guy that is unflappable in most situations, Church makes him fucking skittish. "Nothing too bad, we just really appreciate your family's contribution."

"Pres, it's all good. I don't know if you've noticed this or not, but the Tombs have infiltrated your club. The least we can do is give as much as you do."

"Infiltrated is definitely the word I'd use," I laugh to myself, "Still, it's appreciated."

"I'll let them know. I'm heading home now. We're moving Lovely into my cabin and moving my stuff to Blanche's."

"As much as it pains me to say it, I think living next to Pops will do her the world of good."

"Yep. He may be a few sandwiches short of a picnic, but he's one of the best people I know."

I can't help but nod my agreement. Pops may be the nuttiest bastard I've ever come across, but he's a good man. And I'm damn glad he's on our side.

Pops

"Is there a reason you're just standing around with a big ass tree?" Tav grunts at me. Fucker just turned up and he's already on my case.

"Yeah, I'm fucking old and I'm waiting for your slow asses to get outta my way so I can get this tree into Lovely's new place," I get myself even more comfortable, leaning against the Christmas tree beside me while Tav grumbles. He and Jules are both trying to move a couch into his old cabin, but it's not going well.

"Jules, to the left. The left numbnuts!" He gives me the stink eye and I cackle. God winding these kids up really tickles me.

"Stop it, Sidney, you'll distract them," Debs says, hitting me with her always present dish towel. She comes to a stop beside me, leaning slightly into my side. "I'm going to catch a ride to the clubhouse with Blanche and little Bee. She's bringing Lovely and dropping the kids off to Tav to 'help'." We share a look and then both laugh.

Not two seconds after she mentions Blanche's name, the crunching of tires on the gravel drive marks her arrival. She pulls to a stop and I brace myself for Hurricane Cove.

"POPS!" The kid has absolutely no volume control. "Pops, we're helping Aunt Lovely move into the cabin today," She sings, grabbing my hand and swinging back and forth as she wiggles in front of me. She then drops my hand and gives Debs a cuddle. Elio makes a beeline for Tuesday who is waving like a madwoman at him. Instead of going to help in Tav's cabin, they walk into hers, slamming the door behind them. They make a funny pair, but I know it takes a weight off of Blanche's shoulders knowing that there is someone that understands her youngest.

"Hey Pops," Niko gives me a fist bump on his way past to help the guys, Sage following after dropping a kiss on my cheek.

Today marks the end of an era for us. After being home to all of us Tombs', me in the big house and the kids in their cabins, Tav is moving in with his new family. With his cabin empty we thought it would make the perfect jumping off point for Lovely and little Bee.

"Hey Pops," Lovely says, stepping forward and wrapping her arms around me for a quick squeeze.

"Hey sweetheart, ready for the big move?"

She takes a deep breath and then blows it out, "I think so. I've never really been on my own before, but I think it's time."

"You do know that you'll never be alone here, right?" Jules grunts on his way past us, carrying a crib into the cabin, dodging Rhodie who has his arms full of cushions. Pussy.

"He's right, you know. Once this kid comes out I'll be popping over all the time for advice or just another adult to talk to." Ana says, pointing to her swollen stomach.

All four of my grandchildren are here, as are their partners, well the ones that have partners at least. Jules is still a single unit, but I'm hoping he'll find someone to settle him down soon. Fucker is too old to be messing around with the women he does. If he doesn't stop soon I worry his dick will fall off.

I take in the scene. I never thought we'd have all this. Some semblance of a "normal" life. When I got the phone call that my only child and his wife had been murdered I wanted blood. I wanted to tear apart the men that took them away from me, from us, but instead I had broken kids that needed me. Sure Gus and Jules were older, but losing their parents in that way, and their baby sister being the only witness, somehow solidified them all into one unit. Did I worry that they were all codependent? Fuck yes. But does it make me happy knowing they have each other's backs? Hell yeah.

"Ok Sid, I'm off." Debs pecks a kiss on my cheek and I give her hand a little squeeze.

She's stunningly beautiful and the absolute package. As soon as we met her, everyone in my family fell in love with her. She may have originally arrived as an in-law, but very quickly she softened us up and made us more of a family than we could ever have imagined. We are a couple in that we have strong feelings for each other and enjoy each other's company, but I think she wants more commitment. As much as I want to claim her, and make her my Ol Lady, like the MC kids like to say, I'm on the fence. I'm old and she deserves someone who can keep up with her, not just in the bedroom, but in life. The last thing she needs is to tie herself to a man that could drop dead at any time. I mean, I'm amazed I've made it this far with all the shit I survived in my youth.

"You OK Pops?"

Snapping out of my thoughts I turn to see Lovely's dark eyes, full of concern. "I'm OK sweetheart, just wondering if I'm too old to jump into something with both feet."

She tips her head to the side and studies me for a moment. "Why wouldn't you? You have nothing to lose, Pops, and everything to gain. Besides, it's Christmas, that's when miracles happen." She beams at me, then at her new home, nestled in with the Tombs family.

"You think?"

"Of course! Not that long ago I escaped Eden's Keep. I was running for my life to save my daughter. Now, I have family, friends, and a new home with people I love. I don't think it can get any better than this." She says, a little breathless as she recognizes how wonderful her new life is.

"Well, kiddo, it's going to get better. Trust me," I wink at her before looking at my grandsons standing around. "If you assholes have finished, come help an old man with a tree."

They all roll their eyes but begrudgingly help me wrestle Lovely's Christmas tree into her first home after finding her freedom. Huh, maybe she's onto something. If this timid woman can grab the bull by the balls and make a terrifying choice for a better life, then maybe this old man can too.

Debs

"So, what have we got planned?" I turn to Blanche after checking on Bee in the backseat, nestled in her capsule, fast asleep.

"OK. I told Tav that I had a cheater to watch, which isn't a total lie. My mark works at the mall so I can quickly check in on him while we're shopping. Anyway he thinks I'll be on a stakeout all day, when really we're going on a spree." She waggles her eyebrows at me and I laugh at her.

Blanche is a breath of fresh air breezing into the Tombs family and I'm here for it. She fits in well and I think she may be the ball buster that the family needs every now and then. Don't get me wrong, I love them all, but jeez, do they thrive on chaos and dick punches.

"*Ka pai.* Marx texted me to say the prospects are in charge of decorations and shopping under our watchful eye, so I have sent them on a mission for the clubhouse decorations and the food shopping for our Christmas meal. Nat and Remy are in charge of where all the decorations are going, so I imagine that should be fairly problem free."

"That's good. That leaves us in charge of gifts then?"

"You'd think we'd be all shopped out after finishing the gifts for the community kids, eh?" I say, shaking my head. That was a hectic two weeks, but all the Ol Ladies and I put our best feet forward and cut a swathe through the Rose Grove Walmart's toy section. "We need gifts for the kids, and stockings for both the kids and the brothers. I got these made up," I wait until Blanche stops at a red light before showing her my phone screen.

Blanche takes one look and then throws her head back in laughter, "How the hell did you find someone to make biker boot stockings?"

"I met her at wine and craft night," I snort

"Of course you did." She shakes her head at me and indicates to pull into the mall. "Lovely said that Bee will need a feed in two hours, so I say we start off with the MC stockings first."

"Yup," I agree with her. "I can sit in the food court and feed her while you go and check on Mr Wife Cheater, then we can work on the kids' gifts."

"Yes, but they are only getting one small thing each, got it?" She says, eyeballing me from the driver's side. If I was a weaker woman I'd fall for her intimidating look.

"We'll see. It's both my and Sid's first Christmas with grandchildren. I can't promise anything." I try to placate.

"Try." She says and then rolls her eyes when I laugh at her. "I swear you're going to spoil those kids."

"Yes, but Mama, they deserve it. You all do."

She gives me a look before huffing a breath and then reaching over the console to take my hand. "Thank you, Debs. Truly. Between you and Sid and the whole Tombs family and all you've done for us, we'll never be able to thank you enough."

"Pssh, we're family. It's what we do. Now chop chop, we have stuff to buy."

We get out of Blanche's SUV and while she gets Bee's stroller out of the back, I unbuckle the little sweetie and check to make sure she's warm. Even though Texas can be bloody hot, it's winter so it's cooler out. Too cold for little Bee to be out and about without a hat or a blanket. She's looking just fine in her cute little black beanie with the DRMC logo on the front, and I know under her blanket she's wearing the baby motorcycle boots the brothers got for her. She's one well loved little girl, so I drop a kiss on her chubby cheek and lift her out of the car.

Thankfully because we have Bee with us today, we get a spot close to the mall doors which are sliding back and forth, letting a steady throng of people in and out.

"Come on sweetheart, let's get you all cuddled up and cozy and then blast all your senses with lights, smells and Mariah Carey on repeat," I coo at the precious bundle in my arms, settling her a little before placing her in her space age looking stroller.

"You ready for this?" Blanche says, pulling her shoulders back and readying herself like she's going to war.

"Ready. Let's do this."

Chapter 2

Pops

"Look at all these idiots," I mutter under my breath. Not quietly enough if Takoda's snort is anything to go by. With Tav's measly belongings now in Blanche's house, he's back at the clubhouse on prospect duty. I take a draw of my beer and watch him and Jimmy try for the 40th time to put the lights exactly where Nat wants them. I mean, to be fair, Nat changes her mind every two minutes, but she can do that. The woman is ready to pop at any moment. Let the pregnant woman have what she wants.

"Nat, please, for the love of Jesus, Mary, Joseph and the little donkey they rode in on, please tell me that is the last string of lights?" Jimmy begs from the top of the ladder.

They've strung lights all around the inside of the common room, and I must admit, it does look nice, even with Dayz's dildo's still decorating the walls.

"Yes, Jimmy. That is the last set of lights." She smiles at him as he lets out a sigh of relief. "For the INSIDE," she cackles, her baby bump bouncing in front of her.

"Baby, you're not going outside. It's too cold and you might slip and fall -" Savage's mouth shuts so fast I hear his teeth clack. "Or you can do whatever you feel is best for you. If you want to go outside, baby, then I will be right there beside you to make sure you're safe."

"Aw, thank you baby, you're just so sweet to me," Nat sniffles.

"Is that normal?" Rider whispers to me as he sits his big ass on the bar stool next to mine.

"Totally normal." I reply, eyes still glued to Savage groveling to his wife. I have no idea why it gives me great glee watching this, but it does.

"Remind me never to knock anyone up," he shudders.

"I feel sorry for the poor woman that ends up lumped with you, kid, I really do." I shake my head sadly.

"Hey! I'm fucking delightful!"

"Yeah yeah. Anyway, have you seen Debs? I figured she'd be here getting ready for Christmas and stuff." I check my phone, the text big enough for me to see without my glasses. The kids like to give me shit about it but I dont give a fuck. Hmm, no messages from her, that's odd.

"No, I haven't seen her all day, come to think of it. Huh," He knocks twice on the bar top before taking his beer with him to god knows where.

"She'll be in soon, Pops, she's never late for dinner. You know what she's like. Something would be really wrong for her to miss feeding her boys," Takoda says in that deep as hell voice of his, a smile on his face.

That's the type of emotion Debs brings out in people. Especially people who are lost or lacking the love of a mother. Much like a lot of the men here. Come to think of it, apart from Wire and Takoda, no one else seems to have a mom around. That's the type of thing a shrink would love to look into. Why MC men have no moms and terrible taste in women. Apart from Tav, Rhodie, Wire and Savage of course. Although I don't think those men had much of a choice. Their women chose them, and these guys latched on knowing they'd never find a better woman to love them.

That's when it hits me. I'm just like these men. I have a good woman wanting me and in return she'll give me her heart. And here I am pussying out because I'm old. Well fuck that. I may be old but I'm not stupid. I'm going to do what these boys have done. I'm going to grab on to Debs and love her for the rest of my days.

"You alright Pops? It looks like you've been hit upside the head," Takoda asks, worry etched on his face.

"Yeah, kid. Just had a pretty big boot up the ass, so to speak."

I'm going to make Debs mine. I can't just tell her though, I need to do something big. Something exciting.

"Oh - oh - OH!" Nat's voice gets higher and louder, all of us snapping our heads in her direction.

"Baby, you good?" Savage grips her hand, looking into her face.

"No, I think the baby might be on its way. I've been having cramps all day but this feels different," she murmurs through gritted teeth, her shoulders tense for a moment before relaxing a little.

"Shit, OK baby, just breathe," Savage says gently, then yells almost in her face, "Someone bring Nat's hospital bag!"

There's commotion as brothers stampede around the clubhouse, I'm not even sure what half of them are doing. The clever ones, like Tank and Judge, let us know they're going to bring the club SUV closer to the door, ready to load Nat in. Dex has called ahead to Jimmy to get the gates open and brothers are heading out to their bikes, ready to roll out as soon as Savage and Nat do.

"Here's your bag brother!" Rider says, coming to an abrupt stop in front of Savage and Nat, who's now standing. "Do you need me to drive - what the fuck!?"

Nat's water has just broken in a gush of fluid over his boots and all goes still and silent. Savage and Rider mirror each other with horrified looks on their faces while Nat has burst into tears. Everyone else is absolutely silent. Holding up my hand with my five fingers up I slowly bring them down, one by one in a countdown. By the time I tuck my last finger down Rider's gag reflex has kicked in, snapping everyone out of their shock.

"Let's go baby, let's get you to the hospital," Savage gently leads his wife by the hands, stopping to slap a hand on Rider's shoulder. "Sorry, brother. See you at the hospital,"

"Let's roll out brothers, we got a baby on the way," Marx circles his hand in the air and the brothers start to leave, heading for the hospital.

"Need a ride, Pops?" Rhodie asks, his arm around Dayz who looks less than enthused.

"Not excited Dayz?" I ask, trying hard not to laugh.

"I can't take Chomper with me so he's in his enclosure," she grumbles. She's been obsessed with her gator since she got him. "Also, it's too soon. A first baby can take anywhere from 12 to 24 hours to be born. That's a long time to wait. I'd rather work on my Christmas craft with Chomper,"

My brows hit my hairline, at the same time that Rhodie smiles down at her like the sun shines outta her ass.

"Since when did you start crafting? And how does Chomper craft?" I ask.

"Since I accidentally ordered too many dicks, and he keeps me company."

"Fair enough. Anyway, you two go on ahead, I've got my pickup. I'll drive myself over after I let Debs know what's happening."

"She already knows, Wire bulk messaged the ladies and she said she was on her way," Rhodie goes to drop a hand on my shoulder, and then thinks better of it. "See you there old man."

I nod absently. It's not like Debs to not tell me what her plans are throughout the day. She hasn't gotten sick of me dragging the chain, has she? Shit, I gotta make it up to her. What did Lovely say? Christmas is the time for miracles? Well, I'm gonna plan something that blows generic Christmas miracles out of the water.

"Dayz, do you want to help me with a Christmas thing?"

She raises a brow, "What kind of thing?"

"A big thing,"

"How big?" she asks. Rhodie's head is looking back and forth between the two of us.

"BIG, big."

"Explosions big?"

I think about it for a moment. Explosions always make things better, right? "Maybe,"

She blinks twice. "I'm in."

"Good. We'll reconvene after the birth. Let's go."

Debs

My feet are killing me. We got the first leg of our shopping done fairly quickly. We ticked Rider, Tank, Judge, Fox and Nitro off the list first. Then I got a cup of coffee and fed Bee. She's such a good little girl. She doesn't fuss a lot, and is remarkably quiet. A lot like her mama I guess.

While I fed Bee, Blanche went off to check on the shoe salesman that's been having a little too much fun in the store room with an employee. She's been back for a while now and we've decided to hit a couple more stores before heading home.

"What do you think of this for Dex?" She holds up a face bandanna thing with a skeleton jaw on the front. I've seen the brothers wear these types of things when out on a ride, probably to stop getting bugs in their teeth.

"I think that would suit him, he's a bit of a dark horse and all. Put that in the basket for his stocking. Now, do you think all the boys would like Nerf guns?"

Blanche snorts and then looks at her watch, tapping it a few times. "Whoa, we gotta pack up Mama, Nat has gone into labor!"

I clap my hands in excitement, ditch our basket and speed walk toward the door, using Bee's stroller as a battering ram. We have places to be, people! In no time I have that sweet baby out and in her car seat, Blanche tossing bags and the haphazardly folded stroller into the back of her car.

"Get in lady, we got rubber to burn!" She hollers, starting the engine as I climb in beside her, buckling up as she pulls out of the parking lot like a bat outta hell. "So, what do we think she's going to have?"

I think for a moment, then come to a decision."I think it's going to be a little girl."

Blanche holds her hand up for a high five, "Yup, Savage needs another Nat in his life,"

We both cackle at this and make our way to the hospital, which takes little to no time at all given that we weren't that far away to begin with, and Blanche drives like a maniac. Well, maybe less of a maniac, more of your average school run mum. Quick and efficient with a tinge of NASCAR.

Pulling up to the main doors, Blanche switches the car to park, runs to the back of the SUV, pulls out Bee's stroller and then rolls it toward me. I put Bee in making sure the *pepi* is as snug as a bug in a rug and I push her toward the reception desk, while Blanche finds a parking spot. Before I can even open my mouth to ask for directions to the maternity ward, the frazzled nurse behind the desk speaks.

"Let me guess, you're somehow related to Natalie Clarke?"

I suppress my giggle, and instead grin at her and nod.

"Level 3. I'm sure you'll be able to find the other 100 family members crammed up there. Dr Manning is on duty, so you'll hear all the updates in real time." I suppress a laugh because Dr Manning, Switch, has a voice like a bullhorn.

"Thank you, love. Here," I quickly rummage in my bag, triumphantly pulling a chocolate bar out with a flourish. I place it on the reception desk and push it toward her, her face lighting up.

"Oh you absolute angel! Thank you!" She smiles wide and I give her a wink.

Pushing little Bee toward the elevators I check on her for a moment while we wait for the next available car. A "ding" sounds out when the elevator arrives and the doors slide open revealing a frazzled looking Rider.

"Whoa, are you alright?" I ask, knowing that clearly he isn't. He's somehow green and pale at the same time.

"Nope. Not at all. I'm going to take a walk and think about my life," he mumbles.

He moves to walk around me and I can't help myself. I reach out and pull him into my arms, giving him a tight squeeze. He stiffens up a moment before he curls himself around me, his large hands patting my back gently.

"You're a good brother. You came all this way to support Savage and Nat, and I'm proud of you, knowing how squeamish you are,"

He huffs out a laugh and then lets me go. "Thanks, Mama Debs. It's been a long time since I had a hug like that." He bends and peeks in at Bee, rubbing his finger over her chubby cheek before standing, patting me on the shoulder and then walking off, eating up the floor with his long stride.

"Come on Bee, let's go see if this *pepi* is here to meet us yet." Rolling her into the lift, she gives me a snuffle and a fart before settling down again.

I watch as the floor numbers tick over. I'm glad that I'm familiarizing myself with the hospital now, so I'll know where to go when Ana goes into labor. With her and Nat due at the same time, it'll be a matter of days, rather than weeks before I hold my newest grandchild in my arms. The baby won't be my first, that was Jovie. Then Niko, Sage, Cove, Elio and Bee came along. Savage and Nat's baby will join that pack soon too. Ana and Gus's baby will be the youngest in my list of grandies, and I can't wait. The doors slide open and I see what the nurse was talking about. The waiting room is packed with giant men in leather, the Tombs' and Lovely. As soon as she sees us she swoops in for a hug and then fusses over her baby. I get it, this is the longest she's been away from Bee in her short little life.

"How's it all going?" I ask as she drops kisses all over the sleeping baby's face.

"Good, there's some good noises coming from the room and Switch yelling encouraging words, so it sounds like things are moving along quickly. Rider got a little curious and peeked into the door."

"Lemme guess, that didn't go well?"

A grin stretches across Lovely's face, "Not at all," she giggles. "Come sit, Pops saved a seat for you,"

"Aw, he's such a good man."

"That he is. He growled at anyone who even hovered around it. That's why Jules is sitting on the floor."

I look to where Lovely is pointing and roll my lips between my teeth to stop myself from laughing. Jules is sitting on the floor, his back against the wall glaring at Pops who is glaring right back at him.

"Who's winning?" I ask them.

"Oh babe, you're here, I saved you a seat," Sid says, standing and kissing me on the cheek, his stubble rasping my skin a little.

"Thank you, Sid. But again, how long were you staring at each other?"

"He can stare all he wants, he isn't getting the chair," Sid says seriously. He holds my gaze and in my periphery I can see his hand raise, middle finger up at his grandson.

Jules just shakes his head and looks down at his phone. Of all the kids he's the one I worry about the most. Gus, Tav and Tuesday all found their people, partners that fit them like a glove. I want that for Jules too, but I can see he doesnt think he deserves the same happiness. I don't know what happened to make him think like this, but I'm sure that with the right person, he'll be able to drop those walls and see that he deserves to be loved and so much more.

I take a seat next to, I want to say my man, but we've never really said what we are to each other. I know I have deep feelings for Sid. I've grown to love the wild man, but I'm not sure that he's quite there yet. I know that he worries that he's too old for me, but what's 9 years in the scheme of things? It's nothing. We're not dead yet so we may as well make the most of it.

He grabs my hand and twines our fingers together, giving me a little wink. I squint at him but let him move our entwined hands into his lap. He's up to something. He's acting all weird.

"Are you OK?"

His head snaps around, and he gets that look that Chewy does when she tries to lie to her family. Eyes wide, he tries to smile. "Of course, babe. Just excited for the baby is all,"

I study him a little longer before shaking it off. If there's one thing I know about Sid, it's that he does love babies. Before I can drill him a little more the door at the end of the corridor swings open and Savage comes rushing out, glowing with pride and looking disheveled.

"We have a daughter! She's so fucking beautiful and she has dark hair just like her momma and I think she has my eyes but it's hard to tell," He's giddy with joy and we all rush up to offer our congratulations and hugs. Well, us women give him hugs, the men all do that hand shake back thumping stuff.

"Congrats brother, you deserve all the happiness," Marx says to Savage before turning to the room, "To the newest DRMC member!"

The men all whoop and Savage runs his hands down his face, still not able to wipe off his smile. "Thanks brothers, oh man, it's just, wow. Just fucking mind blowing. A baby girl. What the fuck am I going to do with a daughter?" He starts looking a little pale and the brothers all laugh at him before promising to help him kick any future boyfriend's asses.

Once they settle down Marx slaps the new dad on the shoulder, "Get back to your family brother. I'm leaving Dex here for security, but if you need anything, just text." Dex nods and moves toward his brother and ex-Pres.

Looking around the room at my chosen family I see everyone is moved by the birth of the new member. Fox and Nitro have started handing around cigars, Tank and Judge are collecting takings for the brothers that bet Savage would have a girl. And Ana is sobbing.

"Ana! What's wrong *kotiro*?"

"I'm fucking terrified! Nat made it look so easy, she didn't even know she was in proper labor until her water broke! Then she rolls in here and not even an hour later squeezes out that baby!" she wails. Gus is white knuckling the armrest of the chair on one side, his other hand being crushed by his panicked wife.

I kneel down in front of my daughter, placing both my hands on her thighs and squeeze gently. I open my mouth to offer her support but Sid beats me to it.

"Listen here girl, no matter how scared you are, and how long it takes, you'll come in here when it's your time, do the hard work and at the end of it hold that precious baby in your arms. All the fear and pain will be insignificant to what you feel when you look into the doughy little face of Gus's mini me."

He was doing so well too. Ana freezes for a moment and then bursts into laughter, all her worries melting out of her. OK, maybe he did do a good job.

"You got this sweetheart." He drops a kiss on her head and I hear her whisper her thanks. Gus stands to give his Pops a hug and then wraps his arms around me.

"That's gonna be us soon. I was, am terrified, but knowing that we have all our family waiting out here for us makes me feel better."

Marx's big hand slams down on his shoulder, gripping him tightly. "*All* your family, brother."

Gus stares at Marx a moment before tipping his chin. "All our family."

Marx gives him a little shake, releasing his grip, and then whistles to the brothers who are still milling around. "Let's roll out. We've got Christmas shit to get done."

Chapter 3

Tank

I've been sitting in the club SUV for 10 minutes so far and I'm not sure what I'm waiting for. I spent all day at Devil's Big Tow flip flopping on whether this was a good idea or not. I drum my fingers on the steering wheel for a moment and then think "Fuck it."

I unbuckle my seat belt, get out of the car into the cool weather, slam the door and make my way up the haphazard path, past the metal garden ornaments made to look like old women bending over, their colorful butts up in the air. There's also a bunch of fat gnomes fishing and an ugly bird.

I stomp up the steps onto the little porch, take a breath and knock on the door. There's some bumping going on inside, and some rustling, but no one answers. Leaning to the side I try to look through the window, but my view is blocked by lacy old lady curtains. Raising my hand to knock again, the door swings open abruptly, leaving my hand in the air, fist up.

"Oh hey! It's you, giant biker man. What can I do ya for?" The peppy, kinda odd woman leans against the door jamb, arms crossed over those large tits I never forgot about.

I take her in, from top to bottom and back up again. She's tall for a woman, around 5'10, but still shorter than my 6'3 build. When I met her in the holding cells she was wearing a 1950s type dress. Today she's in soft looking overalls with ladybugs on the front, an old lady cardigan thing and fluffy socks. We may have only spent half an hour, max, in each other's company in the cells, and then again when we had given her a ride home when we were both released, but there was something about her that was endearing. And fun. And weird. I shake those thoughts off and find her staring at me, her brow raised.

"Sorry. I, ah, look, I'm not sure exactly what I'm doing here, but it's almost Christmas and I remember you saying that you didn't have anyone, so I kinda thought, if you don't want to be alone, you are welcome to come to the clubhouse." Fuck. That sounded so bad. Like a teenage, hormonal Tank asking out Kelly Masters in front of the football team and getting rejected.

"Huh. That's nice of you. But I have a thing planned. I'm heading to Vegas to meet up with some writer friends for Christmas. We're going to eat our weight in food and brainstorm new ideas. There's a signing there too so I'm gonna meet some fans, buy some books, take in some strip clubs. If I was in charge of naming a strip club I'd call it 'Titty Titty Bang Bang'. Hmm, maybe I could double my money and make it a strip club come brothel? Is it called a brothel? What's a nicer name? Escort palace?" She squints up at me, searching my face as if I know the answer.

"Ummm, not sure. But anyway, I'm glad you have someone to spend Christmas with."

"Oh yeah, totally! Thanks for the offer though, dude." She smiles big at me, her green eyes sparkling.

"Merry Christmas Writer Lady."
"Merry Christmas Biker Man!"

Marx

"Church!" I bellow out the doors. I wonder if there will come a time when I can just send the text and they all assemble, without the need to gossip like old ladies and have me yelling at them. Probably not.

They all trickle in, Fox and Nitro surprisingly early. Who would have thought that all it took to get them to turn up on time is to kick out the bunnies?

"Alright brothers, what's the status report on Christmas?" I ask, wasting no time.

"All the Ol Ladies' and kids' gifts have been purchased, and kind of wrapped," Tank starts.

"The lights are up both inside and out, and we're picking up the tree tomorrow." Fox adds.

I nod. "Good work. What else do we need?"

"The prospects bought a fuck ton of tree decorations so we'll get the kids onto decorating tomorrow after school."

"Shit, we're doing well, brothers. Even with us being a brother down while Savage is at the hospital with his family." My brothers all nod, seeming pleased with themselves. "Well, if everything is under control –"

The doors bang open as if someone kicked them in. I go for my gun only to hang my head when I get a look at the culprit looking safe and calm. "Can we help you, Pops?"

"Yeah. I have a plan and I need help," he says, wandering into the room, shutting the doors behind him. He then grabs an empty chair and pulls it up to the table, taking a seat.

"Is it going to involve blood?" Judge asks. It's a fair question.

"What? No, it doesn't involve blood. It's a Christmas surprise."

"Will there be any drugging, kidnapping, torture or unaliving of anyone?" I grill, raising a brow.

"It's for Debs."

Well, those right there are the magic words. As soon as Debs' name drops from his lips, we are all on board. Mama Debs is a force to be reckoned with, and in a short time has become the heart of the clubhouse. Under her watchful eye we now have a home, rather than a place to stay. Also, we have full bellies, Mom hugs and someone to whip us into shape when needed.

"What do you have in mind?"

He takes a deep breath and lets it out. "I'm going to be declaring my love and taking Debs as my Ol Lady on Christmas day. I need you all to sing and dance."

"Come again?" my brother Rhodie asks.

"I need you to perform Debs' favorite song."

"Wait, wait, wait, what do you mean by 'perform'?" Switch asks. Loudly.

"Perform. Sing, play, dance, whatever the fuck skills you have to make it special for her. I don't know, make it up." He huffs. "You're grown men and I damn well know that English is your first language. What about "perform" don't you understand? Oh, and I want Rider in charge."

"*Me?*" my SAA squeaks.

"Yeah, you. You seem like the best choice to be the creative director. Don't fuck this up." Pops mean mugs him to get his point across.

"Well brother," I turn to Rider, trying hard to hide my smile. "I mean, as a club we would do anything for Mama Debs, and after all her hard work with the community gift and food parcels, I think she deserves this." My gaze moves from Rider to look at all the brothers. Come hell or high water, we'll be performing for her. Well, they will. I'm the Pres. I can sit this out if I want to.

"Fine. I'll do it, but for Debs, not for you, you grumpy old bastard," Rider agrees. Before thinking for a moment and sitting up straight, "Wait, if we're doing that, what are you going to be doing?"

"Don't you worry about me, kid," Pops says, rising from his chair, tapping his knuckles on the table twice before heading out. He stops in the doorway, and turns. "Thank you, DRMC. She's going to shit when she sees what you've done for her." He tips his head at us and leaves, closing the door quietly behind him.

"There's five more days until Christmas. Looks like you have work to do boys," I slam down the gavel and laugh my ass off as they all file out, Rider yelling that he'll see them at rehearsal first thing in the morning.

Chapter 4

Rhodie

"Babe, where are you?" I've already looked in our room and Wire's closet, and no Chewy. She's not in the common room or the Rev room. I know that she's not at work, because she was in the common room when I went into church.

"I'm here," she says, peeking around the door of one of the spare rooms in the clubhouse.

When my dad, Mad Dog, and his cronies built this place, they had visions that it would be a big MC so they built a shit ton of rooms with en suites, knowing full well that a group of men do not want to be sharing a bathroom.

"What are you doing in there?"

"Nothing." She stares at me, and then she's moved to the side by Pops who shoves his way into the doorway.

"Don't ask any questions Shit Stain. We have a secret mission. We tell you, you'll blab to the brothers."

I frown down at him a moment, "Wait, is this for Debs' surprise? Cos the brothers are on board to make it real good for

29

her."

"Yes, they are. For one part. The second part, the part me and Dayz are coming up with, needs to be a secret because if Marx gets wind of it he'll shit."

What the fuck? "I know he's asked you this already, but are you going to murder anyone, blow up anyone, torture anyone or do anything that will result in danger for anyone in this clubhouse?" I cross my arms over my chest. I'm not his grandson-in-law at this moment. I'm the enforcer of the DRMC.

He and Chewy look at each other a moment, then squint their eyes, mirroring each other right down to the pursed lips. They nod and then turn back to me. That wasn't creepy at all.

"No to all of the above," Pops says with a nod.

"Ok, that's good. Sounds like you might be up to something normal for once." They side eye each other again but I'm not too worried now that I know I've ticked off all the things that would cause my brother to lose his shit.

"Check your phone in a while. I'm sending you a location. I have a surprise for you," Chewy says, waggling her brows at me before yanking my head down, and sealing her plush lips against mine. It's a little uncomfortable because she has Chomper in the front pack and he's wedged between us, but it doesn't stop me letting out a groan when she rubs her hand over my stiffening cock and sucks my tongue into her mouth. The little minx.

"Stop moaning and get outta here, Shit Stain. We got shit to do!" Pops growls from inside the room.

"Go on baby. I'll see you in a bit."

She nods once, walks into the room and slams the door in my face.

I sigh and step back from my woman. Wandering down to the end of the hall I look in to see if anyone is hanging out in the common room. It's fairly empty, although Debs is in the kitchen singing her heart out.

"Hey Mama Debs."

"Hey love, sit over there and don't touch anything. If you can do that I'll give you a cookie." She smiles, the apples of her cheeks pushing up, making her eyes look squinty. It's the best kind of smile.

"You don't have to tell me twice!" I take a seat on the other side of the bench and she places a plate of chocolate chip cookies in front of me. The sweet scent invades my nostrils and I try to eat like a gentleman. Instead I scarf them down like Cookie Monster.

"Good?" Debs asks, her lips curling at the corners.

"The best."

"Rhodie, what do you think Marx's perfect Christmas would look like?" she asks, plopping balls of dough onto a baking sheet.

I wrack my brain. He's always been my big brother, always put together, in charge. I have never once thought about what his hopes or dreams may be. Debs must see this realization on my face because she wipes her hands and then lays one on top of my hand.

"Hey, *tama*, it's OK to not have thought about it before. He's your big brother. I was just asking if there was anything special we could do or give him for Christmas is all." She pats my hand and then gets back to plopping.

"Well, I have noticed that since the women and kids have arrived, he's been a lot happier. I know it's hard to tell because he's always yelling, but I think with the clubhouse full it reminds him of our childhood. When our mom was still alive and there were kids running around with us. I think just having kids sit in the common room around the tree would do it for him. Well, that and, if I share this with you, you can't tell anyone I told you, OK?"

"My lips are sealed. No one will know that you're my informant." She does the universal zipping her lips and throwing away the key signal.

"When we were kids he always wanted a Mr Potato Head." I shrug. I remember him telling me when Santa gave me one for Christmas that he asked for one from the ages of 5 through to 8 and never got one.

A smile grows across her lips before her brow pinches. "What did you always want as a kid but never got?"

"Oh that's easy. I always wanted an Easy Bake Oven because then I could make my own cookies," I laugh. "I never asked for one because I thought the other kids would laugh at me. Kids are dicks."

Debs bursts out laughing, and so do some masculine voices behind me.

"I always wanted a light saber," Fox says, Nitro agreeing with him, because they agree on everything.

Debs holds out plates of cookies to all the brothers trickling in. Some of them were out making deliveries, the rest decorating. "What about you boys? What did you want for Christmas from Santa?"

The guys all start talking over each other, sharing what they had on their Christmas lists and whether they got what they coveted. Marx pulls up a chair beside me, munching down on cookies and watching his MC relax for a moment.

I nudge him with my shoulder, "What do you reckon brother? Is this what you pictured for the MC when you took over?"

He turns to me with a grin, his white teeth peeking through

his dark beard. "Fuck yes. Look at this place, we're finally a family, brother. All it took was an autistic woman and her crazy ass family to bring us together," He shoves a whole cookie in his mouth and then moves to leave the room, but I see him look over his shoulder once more. When I catch the soft look on his face he frowns at me and flips the bird.

I'd give him shit, but my phone buzzes with an incoming text. I smile as I read my girl's message and then check the time. I have 45 minutes to get freshened up and meet her at the coordinates she sent.

Standing, I walk around the bench and drop a kiss on Mama Debs' cheek. "Thank you Mama,"

"You're welcome, sweetheart."

I chuckle a little as I make my way past Lovely, stopping to rub Bee's head, before heading to my clubhouse room. It makes me feel warm when Debs calls me sweetheart. I know it does for the other guys too because we're all the same level of pussy.

I take my time in the shower, even going so far to trim up down below. Christmas is in five days and my girl organized a surprise for me. I'll thank her with my body. I think about using her moisturizer but then think better of it, instead putting on some cologne and making sure I dry everything properly. I don't want damp balls getting musty smelling in my boxers. I throw on some clothes including a hoodie under my cut because it's cold out, and then make my way out to my girl. A little wind therapy on a cool night and then the warm embrace of my girl? Fuck yeah.

With minutes to spare I pull up to a nondescript building in the middle of Rose Grove's more swanky stores. There are Christmas lights twinkling in the store fronts, and there's my

Christmas angel in her yellow helmet, disco lights reflecting off the windows surrounding her.

"You made it!" she says, throwing her arms around my neck and kissing me.

"Of course baby! Now, what's this surprise you have for me?"

She doesn't say anything, just grins up at me, takes me by the hand and leads me to a door I never even noticed. She knocks three times and the door swings open, revealing a big bastard wearing a lace mask.

"What the fuck?" I murmur under my breath.

The behemoth sizes me up and then tips his head to Chewy, moving aside so she can lead me down a long, dark hall.

"Baby, where are we?"

"You'll see," she fucking giggles.

We get to the end of the hall and, with a flourish, she shoves through the door revealing a dim room, lights running along the bottom of the walls, illuminating naked people writhing all over a padded floor.

"Merry Christmas, Rhodie!"

Chewy

He's not saying anything. At all. His eyes are darting all over the room and he's very still. He can't be that shocked at what's in front of him, he's a biker. I've seen some of them fucking bunnies in the main room. Maybe he's shocked at how fancy the sex club is? That's probably it. This place has classy curtains and tasteful lighting. The clubhouse has fluorescents and manky couches.

"Chewy, why are we in a sex club?" His gaze finally finds mine and I soak it in. I love looking at Rhodie.

"I wanted to surprise you. Don't worry, I've booked a room. Come on, I'll show you!"

I take him by the hand, and make a beeline for the room I booked. I went for something different. We always fuck at our cabin, or our clubhouse room or the Rev Room. Tonight I thought I'd try something different. I get to the room with the silver number 3 on the front and I swing open the door, stepping inside.

"Tadaaa!" This time I do jazz hands.

"What in the actual fuck?" he whispers, stepping into the garishly decorated room.

"I booked this room because it's called the 'Romance Room'. Looking around, I see it's not quite as advertised."

The pictures made it look like the movies, where everything looks hazy and romantic. In real life it looks more like a Mills and Boon cover.

"Is that a full sized picture of *Fabio*?" Rhodie asks, incredulously.

I let out a sigh, this isn't quite going the way I thought it would. "I'm sorry, I wanted to try something new, and I've never been in this room but I think this is the place that couples in love would come to play. But it's terrible." I can feel my shoulders slumping and I really feel like getting an ice cream.

"Aw, hey, hey, baby, I love my surprise. Was I a little shocked by the live sex show out there? Yeah, I wasn't expecting that. But this? This is you wanting something new and different for us to experience and I love it. Lets cover Fabio with a sheet and then I'm going to put that whipped cream and chocolate sauce over there to good use," He tips his head to the side where there's a table with roses, feathers, chocolate sauce, strawberries and whipped cream.

"I'll let you use that on me if you let me use this on you?" I reach into my bag and pull out the silicone model I made of his perfect erection with the harness attached.

He stares at it, then at me, then back to his glorious fake dick. He lets out a sigh before looking down at me, cupping my face in his big hands and kissing me softly. He pulls back, resting his forehead against mine.

"Fuck it. Merry Christmas, baby."

Chapter 5

Pops

I make sure to time my visit to the clubhouse at the exact moment that Debs and the other women went to visit Nat and the baby. We're on a tight deadline. I have four days to get Debs' surprise ready and I need these boys to do their part.

Stomping into the clubhouse I'm met with an empty room, not a brother in sight, not even Takoda, who is always behind the bar.

"Where in the fuck are they?" I mumble to myself.

I came here expressly to see how they were getting on with their performance. Well, that and to feed Chomper. Dayz was a little put out that the hospital wouldn't allow him to visit Nat and her baby. Nat's little girl was being stubborn with her breastfeeding, so they stayed an extra night. Everyone is hoping that they'll be discharged sometime this afternoon. In the meantime the women were rallying around to raise Nat's spirits and I'm going to feed my gator grandson and crack the whip on these boys. I'm not having some subpar performance for my woman.

Moving down the hall to Dayz's room I let myself in and check on Chomper. "Hey there little guy. Hungry?"

I head for the mini fridge and pull out the container with Chomper's food. I take out a single piece, then figure that he deserves two, I mean, he's being a good boy and all. Placing them in his little bowl, I watch him sniff them out. When he first arrived here Dayz would hand feed him, but he's put on weight and length and he's thriving under Dayz's attention. He gives me a lazy look and then turns back toward the dog bed that Dayz uses for him. I sit on the floor and mentally check off the things I need to do. So far they seem to be under control. I'll check in on the boys, then I'll head to the hospital and act as further security for all my girls. And they are. Tuesday may be my biological granddaughter, but Ana, Remy, Blanche, Nat, and Lovely, all of them, are my girls. Debs, well, she's my woman.

Dusting my hands off I give Chomper a quick pat and leave, pulling the door closed behind me. Turning, I walk directly into a huge, hard body. Most normal people would flinch and jump back. Thanks to my history I lash out and end up getting a handful of Pres' nuts.

"Let. Go. Now. Old. Man." Marx grunts, glaring down at me, but not moving.

"Fuck, you are a tough bastard huh? That grip has brought many a man to his knees," I muse and then realize I still have his junk in my hand. "Shit, sorry there Pres."

Marx takes a deep breath, then shakes his whole body like a dog. "PTSD?"

"Something like that," I mumble back.

He nods his giant head once, "Look, I wanted to find you to talk about this Debs surprise thing. I got her something you can give her."

Intrigued, I follow him to his office. He walks directly to his chair, rests his bulk and points at a large, flat box on the coffee table. Taking off the lid and placing it carefully on the leather couch, I lean forward and peel back the tissue paper, uncovering a leather cut, with "Mama Debs" on the front.

"Shit, son, she's going to fucking love this," I tell him earnestly, stroking the buttery soft leather.

"We voted in church to give her a cut. She's a special lady, Pops."

"Yip, son. She sure fucking is." I look at him, holding his hard gaze for God knows how long.

He nods once, seeing what he was looking for. "Good. Take care of her and treat her like the queen she is. If you don't you'll have every brother here out for your blood."

"Yeah, yeah, I'm shaking in my boots," I say, dismissively.

Marx shakes his head slowly, but I see the twitch in his beard where he's trying to control his smile.

"Thank you, Marx. For everything," I hold his gaze, so he knows how much I appreciate him and the MC, even if I give them shit every moment of the day.

"Anytime, old man. Anytime."

Lovely

"You know, she's a pretty normal looking baby. I thought she'd look way more mangled," Chewy says as she looks at Nat's baby from over Mama Debs' shoulder.

"Gee, thanks Chewy. It makes my heart swell with pride when

you say such nice things about my child," Nat says as she rolls her eyes.

"You're welcome."

Blanche snorts next to me. When I first met my sister I found her terrifying. She's tough and no nonsense. The opposite of me. But, as we've gotten to know each other better, she's more like a toasted marshmallow. Crusty on the outside, but soft on the inside. I never knew what they were when I was in the Keep, but since I've been out the DRMC family have enlightened me to the joys of smores. And one thousand other wonderful things.

"Also," Chewy continues, "What's the baby's name? We can't keep calling her 'The Baby'."

"We have a name for her, we just wanted to tell everyone when we're back home at the clubhouse," Nat answers, sitting up a little straighter on the hospital bed, her legs crossed in front of her. She looks absolutely gorgeous for someone who birthed a baby two days ago.

Chewy nods at this information, but I can see by the look on her face that she doesn't quite understand why the news is big enough for the clubhouse. She doesn't say as much though. She's a quirky woman, and I like that about her. She's also super clever and has been teaching me to play chess so I can play with Elio.

"So, chickadee, when do you two blow this joint?" Ana asks. She's sitting in a visitor's chair, like me and Blanche, but Remy gave up her seat for Ana's swollen feet.

"The lactation nurse said we're good to go this afternoon. I just have to wait for another nurse to come check on me and sign my papers and I'm free!"

We all clap and cheer quietly while we celebrate. I beam as I look around at my new friends. At the Keep I had no visitors. I had no nurse or fancy hospital bed either, having given birth at home with one of the Keep matrons with me. This is much nicer.

"So, Lovely, how's the new house?" Remy asks from where she's sitting on the floor next to Ana.

I sigh as I try to find the words, but words just aren't enough to describe how wonderful it is. "My new home is, it's everything. It's so pretty, thanks to you all gifting me cushions and throws. I have the best neighbors in the world, too." Ana preens at this, while Chewy and Debs nod emphatically. "Never in my wildest dreams did I think my life could look like this, but I thank every day that it does."

Nat tips her head, her brows pinched as she looks at me. "You don't thank God?"

Blanche snorts and then covers it with a cough. We've had conversations about this. "I have faith in something bigger than us. But I won't call him God just yet." I shrug.

Many horrible things were done in His name at the Keep. I guess in my mind it's easier to move on and be brave by not thinking about Him. When I do, I remember all the lessons from the Council and what my place is in the pecking order. The old Lovely wouldn't be sitting here with friends, and laying her head in her own cabin next to her new family. The old Lovely would be keeping house and making babies with her old, cruel husband.

"That's a good way of looking at it. Although I do invoke God's name. Usually late at night when I'm with my man," Blanche says, waggling her eyebrows.

"We know," pops out of my mouth before I can stop it. I stare in horror at my sister who sits frozen next to me.

I open my mouth to apologize but my sister interrupts me with a loud snort before throwing her head back and cackling like a witch.

"Holy shit, Lovely, I didn't think you had it in ya!" Ana says, giving me a long distance high five.

"Stick with us kid, we'll teach you everything we know," Nat grins with a twinkle in her eye.

The nurse comes bustling in, making moves to examine Nat once more before discharging her.

"How about we get out of here ladies, give Nat some space, *ne*?" Debs says, handing the baby over to Nat.

"Good thinking. The kids will be home from school soon, and they'll be ravenous if I'm not there to feed them all," Blanche says, picking up her bag and throwing it over her shoulder.

"Lovely, I'm on my way home. Want to ride with me?" Ana asks, slowly rising to her feet. I frown at her belly, it's huge in front of her and I'm sure it's looking a lot lower than it was.

"Yes please, if it's no trouble?" I lift Bee in her carseat and hook it over my elbow. She's such a good little girl. She slept through the whole visit, even when the ladies got rowdy with laughter.

"Puhlease. We're going to the same place," she says, rolling her eyes. "Follow the waddler ladies!" Ana says to me and Mama Debs, leading the charge out of the hospital very slowly.

Chewy and Remy follow behind us, and I can hear them discussing whose gifts they still have to buy and how they're going to keep them secret from their Ol Men and the brothers. I smile to myself knowing that I have a little secret, too. I can't wait until Christmas Day.

Chapter 6

Pops

"Welcome," I address my family.

Well, most of them. Debs is busy at the clubhouse this evening, so I called an emergency dinner with my grandchildren and their other halves to inform them of my intentions with Debs. I realized when I was watching the DRMC sing and dance that I hadn't actually told them what I had planned. Well, Dayz knew, but she's not one to gossip. Or pass on any information that she finds "unimportant."

I wait for them to take their seats, all looking confused, but that will all be cleared up shortly.

"Thank you for coming. I have gathered you here for an important announcement."

"Are you dying?" Jules asks, straight out.

"Why the hell would you ask that?" My face screws up cos I'm confused by the shitty question. My eyebrows are pulled low. I can feel it. And see it, what with the long rogue brow hair now in my line of sight.

"You're acting all fucked up," Rhodie says. I glare at him,

mainly because I can't shoot him.

"I agree with Rhodie. Are you sick?" Gus adds.

Why the fuck do they all think I'm dying? "What the fuck are you all on? I'm not sick or dying," Gus relaxes, his body deflating slightly from the release of tension.

"Oh, good. That's good." Gus nods, looking at his siblings, who all mirror him.

"So, if you're not sick or dying, why did you need us? And where is Mama Debs?" Tav cuddles Blanche closer to him, waiting for my answer.

"Well, if you stopped asking stupid questions you would know by now," I huff. "Anyway, I've brought you all here today to inform you that I will be taking Debs as my Ol Lady. I'm going to make it official."

They wait a beat and then all let out whoops. Ana claps her hands and then bursts into tears. Gus pulls her into his side, whispering in her ear. She slaps him away, pulls herself to standing and then waddles over to me, throwing her arms around my neck and crying into my shoulder.

"I'm so happy for you both and I'm so happy for you and Mama." She pulls back to look at me. "I love you Pops, and I love that you love Mama."

I run my hand over her head, and then pull her in for another hug. "Thank you sweet girl, and thank you for bringing Debs into our family. I promise I'll take care of her."

Blanche obviously overheard because she pipes up from her place in Tav's lap. "You better look after her, otherwise you'll have my foot in your ass!" She cackles like the mad woman she is and I have no recourse other than to give her the stink eye.

"I take it you're OK with this?" I ask my grandchildren, looking around the room.

"Am I the only one who thought she already was your Ol Lady?" Dayz asks, looking confused as she bobs side to side, rocking that gator of hers in her arms.

"No, he hadn't made a claim yet, babe," Rhodie answers, dropping a kiss on her head and trying hard to dodge Chomper's mouth nipping at his cut.

"How can he claim an Ol Lady if he's not in the MC?" Dayz frowns, first at Rhodie, and then at me.

"The intent is still the same kiddo. She's mine, and I'm hers." She looks thoughtful for a moment, and then nods, so it must make sense to her. "Also, Dayz and I have a surprise planned for Debs, so keep all your mouths shut and just make sure that she's all relaxed and where I need her to be on Christmas Day. Got it?"

They all nod and chorus their agreement. Well, almost all, Jules tells me that he'll see what he can do. Little shit.

"Good. I'll text you all with the finer details. You can go now."

"Wait, what happened to dinner?" Tav asks, because he's always on the scrounge for food. I thought it would have waned, what with him living with Blanche now.

"I can't feed you, I'm too damn busy! I have three days to get this surprise sorted for Debs." I start shooing them out while they all huff and puff at me but I dont give a shit.

I have to figure out the perfect timing for mine and Dayz's fireworks. I also have to write a speech and take care of some personal grooming. I overheard Fox and Nitro saying how much women appreciate a man with a trimmed bush, and even though I've never thought about it, I think Debs will appreciate the effort. That can be done the night before, I don't want to get too eager and trim up too soon and give her stubble rash or anything.

With that on my mind I make my way upstairs to sort through some things. I never lived in this house with my late wife, or with my son for that fact. After he and his wife died the kids agreed to raze the "murder house" to the ground and start fresh. Though she may never have stepped foot in this house, there are reminders of her, for the kids. I won't remove her from the house, as she has every right to be here, but I will make space for Debs' late husband to join the walls. She told me that in New Zealand the Maori have a "death wall" which is not as morbid as it sounds. The pictures of their loved ones who have passed have pride of place on one wall, pictures of the living not able to be hung with them until they too have passed on to join their family.

Standing in the hall at what I think will make the best death wall, I stare up at the pictures of my wife, son and daughter-in-law. There was once a time where I wished I was up there with them. It's been a long time since I last had those thoughts, mainly because I had four kids who depended on me to guide them through life. I don't think we've done a bad job, the five of us, but I can see how much richer our lives have become in the past year. Finding love, whether it's with a partner or with a group of men who understand us, has definitely been a change for the better. I may have had my reservations in making Debs mine, knowing full well that I will die before she does and I wanted to save her the pain of losing another love, but knowing that she has both my family and the DRMC to get her through it settles any doubt that I had in me.

Now, to make her mine.

Ana

"Oh my gosh I'm so happy and excited for Mama and Pops! Like, how amazing is this surprise going to be?" I say to Gus's back.

I'm days away from giving birth and my waddling has turned from cute, to pissed off duck.

"I'm glad you're happy, sweetness, because as weird as it sounds, Pops will be your new step father," He snorts a little and then lets out a chuckle.

"Nope, he'll always just be my Pops." I huff out. We've walked for 30 seconds and I'm already out of breath. At least we're at our porch. "They've been seeing each other for quite a while, why do you think it's taken him this long to make it official?"

Gus gazes down at me thoughtfully while guiding me down onto the couch. I sit down heavily with a groan and he gently lifts my feet to place them on the ottoman. I try not to look. A few months back I was having lunch with the girls at a cafe in town. I went to raise my feet up, saw how swollen they were and burst into tears. Not the nice, happy kind. The heaving, snotty kind. Dayz left immediately and Remy, Nat and Blanche had to call Gus out of a security meeting to come and calm me down.

"Pops would say it's because he doesn't want to be tied down. But I think the real reason is that he's scared."

I frown up at my big, sexy husband who knocked me up. "Scared of what?"

"He's old. Older than your mom," he raises his hand when I open my mouth,"Think about it, they both know the pain of losing their other half. I would say Pops was trying to spare Debs having to go through it again."

"He's just so sweet," I whisper out, then the tears come and I let out a wail reminiscent of a widow at a funeral.

"Come here baby." Gus sits next to me on the couch, his strong arm curling around my shoulders pulling me into him.

He smells so good and his arm is so muscular and his chest is so hard. He must sense my breathing change because he leans back slightly, tipping my chin up with his finger.

"I love you so much, Ana." he rubs his thumbs across my cheeks, swiping my tears away, then leans down, his lips press to mine gently.

I pull back a fraction, to pull my legs up, curling them beneath me so I can get closer to my husband. I suck on his neck a little, then, like the hippo I am, I try to get my leg over his lap so I can straddle him but this goddamn beach ball of a belly is in the way.

"Do you need me, baby?" his deep voice murmurs, his thumbs gently brushing my tight nipples through my dress.

"Yes, please Gus! I need you so bad." I'm panting and we haven't really done anything yet. I would have thought that I would have given up sex by now, but nope, I still need him to fill me at least once, preferably twice a day.

"Ok babe, on your knees."

He helps position me on my knees, my ass out while I rest my arms along the backrest of the couch. I would be worried about the low angle for him, but I know that he's never skipped a leg day, so I'm sure he'll be fine. If I'm honest I don't really care, I just need him inside me. Now.

His large hands smooth over my arse, down the back of my thighs until they hook under the hem of my dress. Cool air hits my backside when he flips the material up onto my lower back, leaving me exposed.

"Fuck, baby, have you been walking around with no panties on all day?" he asks, his fingers dipping between my thighs, slicking through my lower lips, and circling where I desperately need him.

"Gus, please!"

I yelp when his hand comes down on my left cheek, before his rubs out the sting.

"Answer me, Ana. I want to know if you've been walking around with this sweet pussy uncovered."

I growl, "Yes! My undies keep rolling down my stomach and it's uncomfortable. Happy?"

"Very," he whispers in my ear, the warmth of his breath causing goosebumps to break out down my spine. I feel his large body behind mine, his cock lining up, and then in one brutal thrust he's exactly where I need him to be.

"Hold on baby, this will be quick. You feel so fucking good, I dont think I'll last,"

I nod frantically and hold on, my head lolling back as one hand cups my belly, and the other grasps the back of my neck. I fucking love when he holds me like this. He pulls out and then slams in again and again, and after the fourth thrust I can feel my body racing toward what I was craving.

"Oh God, I love you baby, I love you so much, you feel so fucking good." He groans long and low when I clench down on his cock, my very own groan joining his as his thick cock hits the part of me that feels oh, so good.

"Oh Gus, don't stop, right there, right there!" I scream as he pounds me over and over, his brutal grip sending me higher and higher.

I feel my orgasm building, swirling and clenching in my lower belly before stars burst behind my eyes and my peak barrels through me in wave after wave of pleasure. There are no thoughts, no words, no sights or sounds. It's just me and Gus as one, as I shake around his thickening cock. In one last hard thrust he fills me, stilling behind me and the kick of his cock and the warmth of his cum sets off a chain of little flutters in my pussy.

"Holy fuck babe, you are so wet, it's gushing all over me," he chuckles, kissing me gently on the neck. "Let me get a towel to clean you up, stay right there baby."

The weight of him eases from my back, his cock the last remnant of him with me. He eases back, and with a pop his cock releases, and so does what feels like a torrent between my legs.

"Oh fuck! Babe, are you OK? Fuck, shit, what? Is this? Oh shit, oh shit!" His voice gets higher and higher and I know I need to stop him from spiraling, but my waters just broke on the couch and my naked arse is in the air.

"Gus! Where are your Tums?" I yell at him. His retreating footsteps mean he's left the room for the moment, so I gingerly turn, trying to miss all the fluids from Gus and myself.

I can hear him in the cabin, and he's talking a mile a minute to someone, so I know that we're about to be invaded at any moment now. I don't mind the family being around while I labor, but I do mind that some poor nurse is going to have to examine my vagina and she may still have traces of Gus in and around her, so I waddle my way to the bathroom and strip off.

The twinges across my stomach kick in as soon as the warm water hits it, and I roll my eyes at myself. I've been having these cramps since yesterday, but I figured it was more of those Braxton Hicks things. Maybe I should have paid more attention. And maybe not had hot, hard sex with my husband just before.

"ANA, WHAT IN THE FUCK ARE YOU DOING IN THE SHOWER?

Here we go.

Chapter 7

Remy

"Mags! Ana is in labor! Dad and the big kids are babysitting," I call out to him as I power walk past my sexy man and his bank of computers, to the private side of our Control Center. I pull out a fresh set of clothing and warm up the shower as I strip off my sweaty gym gear.

"Mags! Did you hear - oh." He's standing in front of me, his shirt already lying on the floor behind him, his big hands unbuttoning his jeans. "What are you doing? I have to shower and we have to get to the hospital. Me and the girls are in charge of managing Gus's anxiety."

"All in good time, Retta. The baby won't be here for at least a few hours, and I missed my woman." I can tell he did, because he's pointing straight at me, with the most beautiful cock in the world. "Besides, you just got back from a workout, and you know I love it when you're all pink and sweaty and sticky." He punctuates each word with a kiss along my collarbone as he guides me into the warm water.

He soaps up his hands, running them over my heated skin, paying extra attention to my sensitive breasts. "Gotta get the girls," he whispers and I chuckle. He's my favorite dork.

He turns me to the spray, the running water washing the suds from my body as he gently runs his hands down my back, smoothing over the globes of my ass, a thick finger slicking over my pucker, rubbing gently until an unbidden moan leaves my lips.

"Soon, baby, soon we'll try this little hole," his deep voice murmurs in my ear, before leaving my peripheral vision.

His hands spread my cheeks and then his warm, slick tongue is at my entrance, tasting, teasing. I press back, uncaring that I'm riding his face, the need to come so urgent as he forces my pleasure higher and higher. My body builds toward its crescendo and then it disappears, Wire pulling back before I can reach my peak.

"Mags! I was so close," I whine, my hips still moving of their own accord, searching for release.

"I want you to come on my cock, that sweet, tight pussy choking the cum outta me, got it Retta?"

Wow. I love when he talks dirty. I nod, because what else could I say to that? His big hands move to my hips, turning me so I'm facing him. "Arms around my neck baby,"

I do as I'm told, wrapping my arms around his neck. He grips my ass, lifting me and guiding me onto his hard cock. I go to wrap my legs around his waist, but he shakes his head at me, then moves one arm underneath my knee, my leg hooking over that arm, then he does the same with the other. His hands are gripping my ass, my legs hanging in the breeze, thighs spread wide. He grins down at me and then bounces me as he thrusts up. I gasp at the sensation. Holy bananas, he's going to ruin me if he plans on doing it like this.

"Hold on baby," he whispers and then bounces me over and over again until we are both shaking, sated messes in need of further showering.

Gus

"Ah, dude, aren't you meant to be back there?" Rider points down the hall I've just come from.

Before I can answer, Pops barrels into me, poking me hard in the chest, "What the hell are you doing out here?"

I catch his finger before he pokes me once more, and hold onto it. "Mama Debs told me I had to come out here and have three conversations before I was allowed back in."

Pops squints at me for a moment. "What the hell did you do?"

I wasn't doing anything. Other than asking the nurses if they'd washed their hands. Every time they touched my wife. And I may have eaten three whole packets of antacids.

Pops is still staring at me, but at the moment I'm more interested in what's happening behind him. "What the hell are they doing?" I gape as I watch Fox, Nitro, Sniper, Judge and Tank shuffling from side to side.

"What?" Pops says, then whirls around to look behind him. "Hands up, Fox, they need to be up higher, fingers spread!"

What in the holy hell is happening? Instead of waiting around for answers I take in the room crammed full of DRMC family, spotting the only empty seat. Plopping down into it I run my hands down my face, and take a few deep breaths. I need to pull myself together and get back in there. My wife needs me.

"You OK, brother?" Rhodie asks, sitting across from me with Chewy on his lap. It's then I notice what she's got strapped to her.

"Dayz?"

"Yeah?"

"Is Chomper wearing a wig?"

"Maybe."

I can see the baby harness straps over her shoulders, but where I would normally see Chompers arms and legs hanging out of the front pack, she has a blue baby blanket draped over him, essentially hiding his gator bits. The only thing that would be sticking out would be his head, but there's a brown short haired wig with a beanie perched on top.

"Dayz, have you disguised Chomper and smuggled him into the hospital?" She looks down at her "baby" and then back at me, grinning wide. Even Rhodie has a huge grin on his face, and that's when I notice the bed hair they're both sporting. "Did you two mess around before you came here?"

"No!" four voices sound out, my head snapping to the two couples sitting either side of Rhodie and my sister. Tav and Blanche, and Wire and Remy. Remy red as a beet.

"Um, I'm going to go get coffee, anyone else want one? Blanche, wanna help me?" Remy mumbles and then shuffles off with Blanche cackling beside her.

"Shame on you!" I hiss at Tav, Wire, and Chomper's parents. "This is a sacred time for me and you're sullying it with your sex smell and bed hair!"

"Hold on a goddamn minute, I heard screams coming from your house and I know for a fact they weren't labor sounds," Tav hisses, stabbing a finger in my direction.

"How do you know what labor sounds like?" I growl at him.

"I've watched movies," he says, crossing his arms over his chest.

Looking up I notice Dex and Savage leaning against the wall, smirking. "Can I help you?" I frown.

"Oh don't stop on our account," Flack says, waving a hand at us as he joins his club brothers with a grin on his face.

"Gus? Ana has asked for you." Thank God. Saved by Mama Debs' sweet voice.

Standing, I make sure to flip the bird at whoever deserves it on my way back down the hall, laughter following me.

"Take a deep breath, Gus. She's doing well, she's ready to push."

I nod at Debs and accept her quick hand squeeze before walking in on my sweet, beautiful, demure wife cussing like a sailor and then growling like she's been possessed by the devil.

"Gus get your sweet arse over here right the fuck now!"

I scuttle closer to my love, and grab her hand, holding it between both of mine. Leaning down I press my lips to her sweaty forehead. "You are doing so we-"

"Stop talking, your breath stinks!" She then starts tearing up, "Why does everyone stink? It smells like coffee breath and donuts in here. Why!?"

"I don't know baby, I have no-"

"Not you! Them! Someone who knows something!"

"It's perfectly normal, Mrs Tombs. When a woman is in labor her whole body is on high alert, many women have a heightened sense of smell. You're doing great," the nurse answers, thankfully. "A nice big push on the next contraction, Ana."

Ana nods, giving my hand a little squeeze. "I'm sorry Gus, I don't mean to be aaRRGGGHHH!"

With that she clamps down on my hand and I'm sure I feel something crack. Holy fuck my girl has a strong grip.

"That's it, long push, oh great job honey, I can see baby's hair!" the nurse coo's encouragingly.

"Well grab it by the hair and fucking pull it ouuuuuuuuuu-utttt!" Ana yells while the nurse smiles politely at her.

"I am so sorry," I mutter to her.

"Oh no need, Mr Tombs. We nurses know that we're almost at the end when the cussing starts." She winks at me and Ana growls at her then apologizes profusely as she melts back onto the bed.

"It's OK *pepi*. We are almost there," Debs calmly says, stroking Ana's face.

Ana starts to groan and wriggle a little, then her body tenses, and I know that another strong contraction is coming.

"Ok Ana, big long push," the nurse says patiently.

She leans to look between Ana's legs as Ana makes an almost animalistic noise, her body shaking with the effort.

"That's it Ana! The head is out!" Mama Debs cries.

"Stop pushing Ana, just pant, and on the next contraction your baby will be born." The nurses check to make sure the cord isn't wrapped around the baby's neck or anything and I pant along with Ana, holding her gaze while we wait the short moments before our lives will change completely.

"Push!" Both the nurses and Mama Debs cry and with one last, long push Ana gives birth to our child.

I don't look, not yet. Instead I stare at my wife as she flops back, exhausted with a huge smile on her face.

"Dad, would you like to cut the cord?" I nod, speechless as I take the scissors and cut where I'm instructed.

"Congratulations Mama and Papa, it's a boy." Mama Debs sniffles, as our screaming boy is placed on Ana's chest where he falls silent, his eyes looking up at his mom with just as much awe as she has looking down at him.

Mama Debs kisses both of us, then rubs my son's tiny, dark head. "I'll go let the family know," she whispers, leaving us in a bubble of our own.

"He's perfect baby, so perfect."

"Yup, little Sidney Michael Joseph Tombs is perfect."

Chapter 8

Marx

I don't know how much more of this I can take. With Debs out of the clubhouse my men are taking this opportunity to practice their performance.

"No, no, no, no!" Rider yells pointing at a different brother each time. "There is more hip movement than what you're doing. And we need to be on the balls of our feet. We. Need. To. Get. This. Right." He punctuates each word with a clap.

My men all stare at him and I know that if this wasn't for Mama Debs they would be laying into him and his dictator ways. Pops really knew what he was doing when he put Rider in charge. The sly bastard.

Rider circles his finger in the air and nods at Cove to press play on his phone, the music piped in through the speakers. I watch them bumble through the routine again and I can feel my stress levels rising. I told myself I wouldn't get involved. Rider is in charge and that takes a load off my shoulders. I already have the club's paperwork to finish signing off on before I can have a short Christmas break.

"Wow, are they getting worse?" Switch asks, using what Cove calls his "outside voice".

"Some are. Some have gotten better. Fox can actually turn the right way now."

We both stare at the men spinning in the common room. Tank accidentally bumps into Judge who then shoves him into Dex's path. Dex sends a death glare Tank's way.

"Well, I'm glad I don't have to learn those moves." Switch shrugs.

I turn to look at him. I had wondered why I didn't see him out here as much as the others. "Why not?"

"Didn't you hear, Marx? I'm going to be the star!" He throws his head back and laughs, heading back the way he came.

"This isn't working! I can't be next to Tank, he has two left feet and he's cramping my style," Dex says, the glare still on his face.

The Ex Death Riders have mixed seamlessly with the DRMC brothers, however, the more I get to know Dex, the more I realize what a perfectionist he is. Similar to Sniper, but more social. Speaking of Sniper, he's managed to nail all his moves, and now he's at the back of the group leaning on the bar, waiting for the next piece of choreography. If the guys in front of me can ever nail this first piece.

"Hey, Uncle Marx." I can tell by sheer volume that it's Cove speaking.

Looking down at her I notice Jovie and Elio on either side. "Hey kids, what cha up to?"

"We were looking for a big person to help us decorate the huuuuuge tree. I've never seen one so big in my whole entire life!" Jovie exclaims, her eyes huge as she takes in the naked pine in the corner of the common room. The top is folded over some because Rider got excited and bought the tree we "deserved", not the tree that could fit.

"Where are the Bigs?" I ask them, usually if Mama Debs, Blanche or Remy aren't around, the big kids look after the littles.

"They're doing boring teenager things," Cove says, nodding at Jovie who shrugs and nods up at me. Elio standing quietly, tracing a pattern on the wall with his finger.

"Well, we can't have a naked tree, can we? Come on, let's go see what decorations the Ol Ladies have left us, huh?"

The girls squeal and fist pump while Elio stares up at me and nods. His gaze moves to my hand, and then back up at me, so I hold my hand out in invitation. I've noticed that the boy is not only quiet, but not a huge fan of touching, so when he puts his warm, slightly damp hand in mine it makes me feel about ten feet tall and invincible. Paperwork can wait for another day.

We wander over to where the girls have started taking brand new tree decorations out of the shopping bags. I remember doing this as a kid with my brother, and dad would have a fit because we'd tear the bag open like feral animals, glitter and crystal raining down on us. But these are two little biker princesses, so they carefully remove everything, cooing over each decoration. They seem to especially love the little motorcycle ornaments, and have decided that Jovie's will be the purple bike, Cove's will be the pink bike and Elio's will be the blue one. He nods so I figure he must be happy with this arrangement.

"OK, Uncle Marx, we'll do the low branches cos we're little. You do up the top cos you're big," Cove bosses. "But don't put them all together, you gotta space them out. Understand?"

I hide my twitching lips from her and nod my head seriously. "Got it."

Elio gives me a funny look that makes me think that he doesnt think I've got it, but I don't let the kid unnerve me. I've been decorating trees since I was their age. I may not have done it in recent times, but I'm sure it'll all come back to me.

"What the hell are you doing? Everyone knows the heavy ornaments go on the bottom." My brother takes the big, sparkly bauble down from where I put it, and moves it to lower down the tree.

"Get away fucker! I got this." I grumble at him. I don't want the kids hearing my bad language. Not because I think it'll offend them, more because they'll demand money for the swear jar the girls made. It sits proudly in the middle of the hatch between the kitchen and the common room, in the perfect place for brothers to be putting money in every time we get pulled up.

"You're doing it wrong!" Rhodie fires back.

"I am not! I've always decorated like this, even before you were born so piss off and annoy someone else," I hiss at him. He narrows his eyes and slowly reaches up to pull another of my well placed baubles from the tree. "You better not touch that," I grit out.

"Or what?" Rhodie challenges, his brow raising.

"I'll tell Chewy that the first time you got drunk you cried because you thought you were dying and then you shit your pants and refused to take them off because you didn't want people seeing your weird balls."

Rhodie's eyes flare for a moment before narrowing at me. A smirk slowly spreads. "Too late, she already knows."

"Yeah, but we didn't," Savage cackles, some of the other brothers joining in.

Rhodie squares his jaw, his eyes dart to the tree, then back to me. "Don't do it brother," I warn him, but I can see the look that he used to give me when we were kids, the look that says he's most definitely going to do what I warned him against. He raises his hand up, fingers brushing one of my baubles. Quick as lighting he snatches it off the tree. Oh it's on!

We shuffle around the tree, shoving and pushing, him trying to remove my baubles, me trying to keep them up there. The brothers are yelling their encouragement, the kids are jumping up and down yelling and my brother and I giggling and snorting like little kids.

"Oh no, watch out!" Jovie shrieks and the tree lurches sideways, then teeters before taking me and Rhodie to the floor.

"What the hell is going on in here!" I know that voice. That's Debs' Mom voice.

"Nothing!" Me and Rhodie both yell out, then look at each other and burst into laughter.

"You lot, get that tree off those boys and help them pick up this mess. Kids, follow me for some hot chocolate and once the tree is back to standing we'll decorate it, *ne?*" The kids nod, and start to follow behind, not before Jovie stops to stand at mine and Rhodie's heads. She looks down at us, her hands on her little hips and she shakes her head slowly back and forth.

Rhodie side eyes me, his lips twitching, "Sorry for being silly, Jovie."

"It's OK Uncle Rhodie, shit happens." She skips off into the kitchen with Wire huffing after her.

Rhodie slides out from under the tree, stands then offers me his hand. "Come on brother, we better put this shit back before we get told off again." He snorts and we join the rest of the DRMC in picking up all the mess before our clubhouse Mom comes in here and kicks our asses.

Debs

I shake my head at those boys and try to keep the smile off my face. It was actually nice to see Marx let loose and have fun. He's been so tightly wound for such a long time, trying to keep the club safe that I was starting to worry about him. Well, him and Gus, because love him as I do, that man is a walking aneurysm waiting to happen.

"Here you go my *pepi*," I place the hot chocolates, with extra marshmallows on the bench and the three little kids all climb up on the stools to sit.

"Anymore where that came from?" Smiling at Sage and Niko I wave them over.

"You know I wouldn't forget my Bigs. Or you, Lovely," I nod over at Lovely who's just inside the doorway, Bee strapped to her front, much like how Chewy carries Chomper.

I pour four more mugs of hot chocolate from the huge pot on the stove, and join the kids and Lovely.

"What is your most favorite Christmas, Mama?" Jovie asks, her tongue swiping over her top lip, completely missing the chocolate mustache.

I think back through all my Christmases. The ones where it was just me and Mick, celebrating on our own and wishing for a child. When Ana turned up on our doorstep, all surly and stubborn, convinced that families don't last for kids like her, well Mick was beside himself with excitement. He decorated the house like his life depended on it. We tried not to give her too many things, not wanting to overwhelm her, but it was hard not to when every time she opened a present her face would light up before asking us if she could keep it forever. She was a suspicious little thing, but with every Christmas after that she realized that we were her family, and she got to keep us forever. Once she was old enough she and Mick would send me out shopping for the day and put up the decorations together so they could surprise me when I got back. They were two peas in a pod. My Ana was a total daddy's girl. When he died it broke Ana in ways that my mother's love could never fix. Well, not until she met Gus and in turn Sid. Sidney treated her in the same way her dad did, so I know exactly why she named her little boy after him, her dad and Gus's dad.

"Hmm, I think it was the first year my Ana came to live with us. You know that Ana wasn't mine from when she was a baby, right?" The kids nod at me.

"Yup. Only Niko and Bee come from their mommy's tummies" Cove says matter of factly.

"That's right! Ana is just like you all, she found me when she was younger. Our first Christmas was my most favorite Christmas. She didn't think that Santa was real because he could never find her house before. But that year, he found her alright."

"A Christmas miracle," Lovely whispers.

"Exactly! A Christmas miracle." I nod.

"Santa couldn't find my house either, do you think he'll find me this year?" Jovie asks, her face full of hope.

Lovely nods emphatically, "He definitely will, Jovie. Everyone knows the DRMC. If he gets lost he will ask someone for directions and they'll help him find the clubhouse," she says, smiling down at Jovie. "Wait, Mama Debs, you said Ana's first Christmas *was* your favorite. Is there an even better one?"

"Yup. It may not have happened yet, but with my new family and the new babies, I think this Christmas might be my absolute favorite."

The kids cheer, chatting amongst themselves that they think this Christmas will be "epic" and all sorts of other hip words. Lovely beams at me, softly jiggling Bee in her front pack. Watching her juggle the little girl with ease I wonder what she'll do as Bee ages.

"Lovely? How long can Bee last in her carrier like that?"

Lovely glances down at Bee's dark, downy head, a little crease between her brows as she thinks. "I think it goes up to around 6 months old, maybe 9 months depending on the baby's size. By then I'll probably have to push her in a stroller a little more. Why is that?"

"How big do you think Chomper is?"

A smile spreads across Lovely's face.

"What are you two grinning at?" Tav asks as he wanders in and drops kisses to the tops of Elio, Cove and Jovie's heads, fist bumping the big kids.

"Are you on prospect duty?"

"Yup. Do you need something?"

"Yes, a ride to Walmart," I grin as Tav groans and his body goes all floppy. "Chop chop, Mama's on a mission!" I cackle as I grab my bag and head out.

Chapter 9

Pops

I park my truck in its usual spot in front of the clubhouse and make my way around the back. I'm feeling pretty fucking special after spending the morning with my youngest great grandson. Not only did Ana gift Gus with the most perfect little boy, but she gifted me with the greatest honor, giving the boy my name. Although we did agree to call him Junior for now seeing as Debs calls me Sid and it would get damn confusing otherwise.

Speaking of, I haven't seen my woman that much in the last few days, given how busy we've both been in the run up to Christmas. And I'm sneaking around planning this surprise for her. We've been talking on the phone every day, but I may have been purposely avoiding her a little. Only because she can read me like a book and I know I'll accidentally give away what I have planned. And what I have planned will blow all other Ol Lady proposals out of the water. Both literally and figuratively.

It tickles me so much that I whistle a peppy little tune as I catalog all the things I need to do. I need to stop by the gym to check on the guys' progress for the performance and then I have an important meeting with Chewy to go over our display and then we'll get to wiring our fireworks, making sure to program the music and the ignitions for full impact. We may have to make them less explosive than I was hoping as Ana, Gus and Junior will be home tomorrow. Having Junior and Savage's unnamed baby around for the surprise on Christmas Day means I don't want anything too loud. We don't want to scare them or anything.

"And five, six, seven, eight!" echoes from inside the gym, music blasting.

My feet hurry me along in that direction to check on the boys' progress. Peeking through the door I'm impressed by what I see. All the brothers except for Marx and Switch are busy going through their steps. Rhodie with that damn gator strapped to his chest, Chomper's arms and legs flapping in the breeze. It may be clunky, but they move in time, the choreography well learned. Sure some are better dancers than others, but that doesn't matter. What matters is these boys are putting everything into this thing for Debs and I couldn't be prouder. I won't tell them that, though.

"Looking good, Dipshits. You might be able to take over from those strippers at the club in Roxburgh!" I yell through the door before letting it slam behind me, silencing their smart ass comments.

Giggling like a little girl, I make my way toward Dayz and my home away from home, the Rev Room. That's where all our tools live and where we can brainstorm new and exciting ideas. I never in a million years would have thought that all the shit I went through in 'Nam would give me the tools to build a close relationship with my granddaughter, and yet here we are.

Swinging open the door and stepping in, I take in the scene

before me. Dayz is bent over the table, her messy bun lurching dangerously close to Elio's dark head, who is also bent over, staring intently at what she's showing him.

"Hey gang, what are we doing?" I ask, stepping closer to the pair.

"Oh, I'm showing Elio the circuit board where we will time all our explosions."

Elio looks up at me when I smooth my hand over his head, giving me a little smile. I feel like a fucking star knowing that Elio doesn't dish out smiles easily. "So kid, are you our new apprentice?"

He turns to look up at Dayz, who gives him two thumbs up. He turns back to me with an even bigger smile and mimics her two thumbs up.

It's funny, because I remember doing this exact same thing with Dayz a long time ago. My son and daughter-in-law never really knew what we got up to in our back shed together, and I'm fucking glad of it too because they would have shit themselves. Now I'm doing it in an even bigger back shed with the next generation.

"Right, first things first, Elio. Safety. We need to make sure we have all the right protection on."

He nods solemnly, then lifts the goggles Dayz has placed in front of him. They're a few sizes too big, so I make a note to ask Tav to pick some up while he's out shopping with Debs. My woman. I feel a little giddy at the thought.

"Strap em on, kid. Shit's about to get real serious in here."

Blanche

I flop down onto my couch, arm across my eyes and savor the quiet. All the kids are at the clubhouse doing God knows what. As someone who has spent the whole of my children's lives being the only person for them to rely on, it seems odd to just be able to leave them somewhere and know that they're safe and happy. It also shows how much easier getting their Christmas shopping is. One full day on Christmas Eve's Eve and I'm done. All gifts bought and wrapped and packed up to be placed under the club's tree. I'm a goddamned Superwoman.

"Babe!" Tav calls as he stomps through the door. I can hear his boots hit the trim from where he's kicked them off.

"In here!" I yell back, my feet in too much pain from my shopathon. You would think that I would have had everything I needed after Mama Debs and I went out the other day, but you would have thought wrong. That stuff was for the brothers. Today's stuff was for the kids and my brothers who are due to descend later this evening.

Tav steps into the room and I have to bite my lips to not burst into laughter. "What the hell happened to you?"

"Mama Debs happened," he sighs as he plops down on the couch next to me, his hard thigh pressing up against my soft one. Usually this would make me horny, but not today. I'm far too tired.

Tav must feel the same because I watch as he looks at our thighs pressed together, and then down at his lap. "She ruined me! I can't even pop a chubby because I'm exhausted!" He flops his head on the back of the couch and pouts.

"Come on, it can't have been that bad. What did she even

need? She got most of all she needed the day Nat gave birth. I was with her."

"Yeah but that was before she decided that Chomper was going to grow too big for Dayz to wear which means that he will need his very own special stroller. That then had to be customized especially for him so we had to go to," he shudders and then whispers, "Hobby Lobby."

A gut busting laugh bursts out of me and can't help but snort and hiccup at Tav's misfortune.

"Yeah, yeah, yuck it up. I swear it was the most trying assignment I've ever had in my life. I'm amazed I still have an intact Achilles tendon! The women and their trolleys were ruthless. RUTHLESS!"

I try to calm myself a little, so I can at the very least pat my man on the shoulder and tell him he's done a great job, but unfortunately I'm leant over the side of the couch with tears streaming down my cheeks. He just huffs and crosses his arms over his chest to wait me out. Poor man.

"Ok, Ok, I'm good. Phew, Ok. Do I even want to know what she's going to do to this stroller for Chomper?" I ask him once my breathing calms.

"Don't know and I don't care. Remy, Nat and Lovely were going to help her, so I'm sure it'll be nice and ridiculous."

I clap my hands "God I hope so!" I grin at him and he rolls his eyes.

Tav looks around, then cocks his head slightly, as if listening out for something. "Where are the kids?"

"They're at the clubhouse. They were decorating the tree and then Cove and Jovie had secret Christmas stuff to do, the big kids were hanging out, and Chewy and Elio had plans." At this, Tav's eyes narrow.

"What kind of plans?"

"Not sure. They were waiting on Pops when I left," I shrug. Tav's brows fly up and he looks conflicted.

"What's wrong?"

"Do we really trust Pops AND Chewy with Elio?"

My brows pinch in as I take in his concerned face. His very handsome, concerned face. "Well, yeah. They're his family. I'm sure they're fine. I mean, what could they possibly be doing? They're working on Deb's surprise."

"Well, I guess. I mean Pops did say that there wasn't going to be any blood or torture or killing, so I'm sure they'll be fine. They're probably making up a soundtrack or something." He looks at me for reassurance and I nod encouragingly at him. "Yeah, you're right baby. We can definitely trust them."

He relaxes back into the couch, positioning himself down one end, leaning on the arm rest, and then taking one of my feet in his hands, tugging on my leg until I'm at the other end of the couch, mirroring him.

"What time are we picking up the kids?" he asks, rubbing the ball of my foot, drawing a groan out of me.

"Mmm, in three hours. That feels so good, babe."

"Well, Pixie, we have two options," he gives me a salacious grin, over my foot. "We can get naked and fuck on the couch, the one piece of furniture we haven't christened,"

"Or?" I raise a brow.

"Or, we rub each other's feet until we fall asleep right where we sit."

"Is it bad if I say we have a nap?"

"Oh thank fuck, I was hoping you'd choose that," he says on an exhale, lifting his socked man foot up so I can pull it into my lap and very half assedly massage it. "I love you so much,

Pixie."

"I love you too, babe."

Chapter 10

Remy

"Mom! Dad! It's Christmas Eve!"

It's also really early in the morning, but it doesn't stop Mags beaming at me, his eyes still closed.

For a long time Jovie called us Retta and Mags, which are the nicknames we have for each other, but recently, in the past month or so, we've been Mom and Dad and I can't help the warm gooey feeling I get when I hear our daughter call us that. Even if it is the crack of dawn.

Jovie bounces up onto the bed, careful not to knee or kick us, and then wiggles under the covers, moving around until she's squished between me and Mags, her silk bonneted head resting in the slight gap between our pillows.

"Christmas is coming tomorrow!" She squeals and kicks her feet under the covers.

"Sure is kiddo. I'm super excited because I've never had a DRMC Christmas," I say, booping her nose.

"Me either, AND Mama Debs and Uncle Marx said that Santa

will be able to find me this year so I will have presents to open!" Her little hands come up to cover her mouth and she squeals into them, happiness vibrating through her.

I grin at my man as he grins back to me. Jovie isn't going to believe her eyes tomorrow morning. Even though we, Blanche and Tav have told all the brothers that the kids don't need much, I'm sure they'll have a mountain of gifts to open and this year I'm OK with that. It'll make up for all the Christmases that Jovie missed out on. I'm sure that her mom tried really hard to give her the world, just as I'm sure her dad would have frittered it all away.

Tuning back into what my daughter is saying, she lists off all the things she has to do today to get ready for tomorrow. "I have to wait for Cove and Elio to get here cos we're going to be baking cookies for Santa. Santa wrote us a special letter that says that he will need lots of cookies to fuel up, and he said that he's lacnose inlorent so he can only have beer."

"Really? Santa told you this?" Mags asks, his brow raised.

"Yup. He wrote a letter and asked Uncle Rider to deliver it to us," she nods, in all seriousness. "So we're gonna make cookies and then we're gonna ask Takoda for some beer. Oh maybe he has a special beer for Santa!"

"I'm sure he does baby girl," Mags nods, rolling his lips between his teeth so as not to laugh at how exuberant she is.

"And then me and Cove have a special surprise that we're working on. And then Cove's uncles are coming and maybe they'll have some gators for us to pet and then we're going to visit with the babies and then we're having a sleepover so we'll have to go to bed early so Santa can come."

"Phew, what a busy day baby! No wonder you're up super early," I say, pressing a kiss to her forehead.

"Yup, that's why I need Dad up now so he can do my hair and help me get ready for the day."

Mags lets out a tired sigh before rolling out of bed and lifting a giggling Jovie up onto his broad shoulder. "Come on Princess Jovie, lets go do this mop you call hair and get you ready for your busy day,"

"Bye Mom! I'll see you later, love you!" She giggles (their way?) out of the room.

I wave and call out my "I love yous" and lie back, smiling to myself. Last Christmas I was a single woman, in a not so happy MC. This year I'm with the love of my life and I'm a mom to the most amazing little girl in the world. Maybe Lovely is on to something with her Christmas miracle talk after all.

My mind drifts off and I must have been mulling things over longer than I thought because Mags comes in and snuggles in behind me.

"I can't wait to see baby girl's face tomorrow morning," he smiles.

"Me neither. She deserves everything and more." He nods in agreement with me. "And you're all set for her big present tomorrow?"

"Yup, it's all cleared with Marx and it turns out that Sniper has experience with training so we're all set."

I flop around until I've rolled over and I'm face to face with my handsome Ol Man. "She's going to shit, as Pops says."

Wire chuckles, his large body vibrating the bed "She sure fucking is. Anything else on her Christmas list that we've missed?"

I shake my head at him, and he smooths my bangs out of my eyes. "Nope. She only asked for three things. And we've got them all, so we're good to go."

"Good. What about you, you haven't given me your list, and it's Christmas Eve. It's like you want me out there fighting feral last minute shoppers."

I press my lips to his in a soft, sweet kiss. "Everything I want for Christmas is right here in this building."

"Love you Retta."

"Love you too Mags."

Jovie

"I never thought you were gonna get here!" I yell to my friend. I've been waiting for aaaaages. I've already eaten breakfast and read to Bumpy my dinosaur and played on my tablet AND filmed a Tiktok with my uncles.

"Sorry, I had to wait for Sage to get out of the bathroom before Mom would bring me. She takes ages to put on her makeup." My friend rolls her eyes at me and it makes me giggle.

"Hi Elio," I wave at Elio and he waves back. He doesn't talk much but I like him because he's clever and has good ideas.

Looking around the big room all the adults are talking to each other. Mama Debs and my mom and Cove's mom are talking to Aunt Nat and the baby. They said they're going to tell us the baby name today when Ana and her baby get here. Then we can say hi to all the babies at the same time. I think that's a good plan.

"Let's go to my tent and we can work on our surprise," I wave Cove and Elio to my room and we crawl into my Rug Rats tent. It's so cool. I love it because my mom had one when she was little too. "Don't forget we have to use our quiet voices," I tell Cove, cos she talks loud, like Uncle Switch.

"We need a plan," Cove says using her best whisper voice.

"Yup. So first we need to ask a grown up to take us to the shops," I reply.

"It has to be a bell shop," Elio says in his soft voice.

"Can it be a shop that sells bells? Cos I dont think there is a bell shop." My face screws up.

"Lets Google it," Cove says to me.

I wake up my tablet and go straight to Google. I'm seven and I'm getting pretty good at spelling so I put in "Bell Shop" and then look at what it says. Some of the words are too big so I switch it to read to me, like my dad showed me.

"OK. It says we can get them at the motorbike shop. That's easy. We just need someone to take us."

Cove looks at Elio and he nods his head. "We could ask one of the prospects? They take people places. Or we could ask Niko. Then him and a prospect could take us and we can buy the stuff when they're looking at bikes. Niko is always looking at bikes." She rolls her eyes. Cove always rolls her eyes.

"That sounds like a good plan. You ask Niko. I'll ask Takoda. Elio, do you have the swear jar?"

He nods and pushes it over to me.

"How much money is in there?"

"$877," Elio says. I'm real glad he's good at math because I don't think me and Cove could have added that all up.

"I think that will be enough. Let's go."

We crawl out of my tent and head to the common room. That's where all the grown ups are. Even Uncle Gus and Aunt Ana are there with the new baby, I think his name is Junior. We all go that way so we can peek at him. He's way bigger than Aunt Nat's baby, and he's real hairy too. We all say hi to both the tiny little babies and then when all the moms are busy talking about baby stuff Cove finds Niko and me and Elio go to the bar where Takoda is.

"Hi Takoda."

"Hey Jovie and Elio. What are you two up to?" Takoda smiles at us.

"We were wondering if you could please take us to the motor-bike shop. We want to buy some presents for everyone."

"Oh, well I'm not sure. I'll have to ask your moms first," he says.

"No, they said it's OK. Niko is coming with us." I point to Niko who's walking toward us with Cove. Cove gives us the thumbs up which means he's going to come with us and our moms won't shit when they find out we've gone.

"The Littles said that you're OK to take them shopping as long as I come along."

"I'm good if you're good," Takoda says. It's some man talk thing I think.

"Yeah I'm fine with it. They only want to go to one shop." Niko says, making his eyebrows go up at us. We nod back and he shrugs.

"Alright then, grab your coats kids and meet me outside."

We all fist pump and dance around, even Elio does, pumping the swear jar in the air. Now we just gotta find the right bells for all my uncles and then help each other wrap them and put them under the tree. I can't wait for them to see our presents!

Debs

I'm exhausted after a long day of baking and preparing tomorrow's menu. Not that I'm on my own with it, no way. Marx had given me the prospects and anyone else that had any cooking prowess, or at the very least could follow instructions. We've gotten everything prepped, anything that could be premade is sitting in the fridge and now we're all sitting in the common room, enjoying some eggnog. We're waiting for Savage and Nat to make their baby name announcement before we gather up all the kids, set out Santa's treat, get them all ready for bed, and then settle ourselves in for the evening. Phew!

It's a full house tonight with all the Tombses staying in the spare rooms. Wire's mom is staying the night so she can enjoy Jovie's first DRMC Christmas. The Landry brothers are also here, wanting to celebrate with their sisters and nieces and nephews. They're staying outside in their RV because their gator Gretchen gave birth recently and they're looking after one of the babies. Marx has already put his foot down and Chewy isn't allowed to go anywhere near it. She already has Chomper, who the Landrys thought was hilarious as he sat quietly in the front pack that seems to go from Chewy to Rhodie and then back again depending on who is doing what.

"You need to move your boy away from my girl," Savage growls out, for not the first time this evening either.

"I'm not moving anywhere! Tell your daughter to stop making eyes at my son!" Gus hisses back as both their women roll their eyes.

"You know babies can barely see further than their hands, right? They physically cannot see each other. Even if they have exceptional baby eyesight, all they'd see is a blob in a blanket," Chewy pipes up, both new mothers scowling at her. She doesn't care, she's busy stroking Chomper's rough skin.

"Savage, you said you had an announcement?" Marx asks, getting everyone back on track.

"Yes." He stands, his baby girl nestled against his chest, his tattooed hand rubbing her back gently. "We know that many of you have asked what we named our little girl, and I wanted you all to be here when we told you." He looks down at Nat who smiles up at him lovingly. "We thought we knew MC life, we'd lived it long enough. We had a family, albeit a dysfunctional one, but one we loved nonetheless. Then we came here and saw how family works when it functions properly and well, we wanted in on that." He chuckles, Flack and Dex whistling at him. "You're all not only family to us, but you're family to our daughter, and it seemed fitting to name her after the MC that changed our lives for the better."

"Even if we do still unalive people from time to time?" Marx asks with a smirk.

"Warts and all, brother," Savage grins back. "We named our daughter after the Devil's Rose MC. Everyone, meet Rosie Clarke."

Everyone whoops and hollers and the two babies just snooze as if nothing too exciting is going on.

"Thank fuck, I thought he was gonna say they called her Devil Rose," Sid's gruff voice whispers in my ear, his warm breath sending a thrill skittering through me.

I turn and smile up at him. "It feels like I haven't seen you in an age, Sid."

He pulls me in for a cuddle and makes a grumbling noise. "I know babe, this Christmas shit is for the birds. I've been busier than I've ever been before. "

"Well, tomorrow you can relax and enjoy watching the kids open presents and eat all the food me and the prospects have been preparing."

"As long as you promise me that you'll be relaxing next to me. Let the prospects do the rest of the work."

"I don't know if they're ready to run the ship alone."

"Fuck 'em. You need to take care of yourself babe. If you won't take care of yourself, then let me."

I gaze up at him, his whiskey colored eyes, so much like his grandchildren's twinkling down at me.

"You're so sweet," I cup his rough cheek, stroking it with my thumb.

"Only to you because I want you around for as long as I can have you," he quietly replies.

My head tips back as I stare at him. "Whatever happened to 'You need to find someone young who won't up and die on you'," I ask, mimicking his deep voice.

"Oh, I still believe you need to find someone younger. You've already lost one love, I don't want you to lose another."

My eyes narrow at him. "What makes you think I love you?" I'm working overtime to keep the smile off my face.

"How could you not? I'm a fucking catch!" he says in the outlandish way only Sidney Tombs can, making me burst into laughter. "Come on you. Everything in here is sorted and clean, the kids have put out that huge plate of cookies and beer and their parents are getting them ready for bed. The new families have already gone to their rooms for the night and everyone and everything is under control."

I gaze around the sparkling kitchen, everything put away for the night. I know full well that everything is prepped and ready to go for tomorrow. Looking through the hatch into the common room there's only Fox, Nitro and Jules out there, probably getting ready to head to town to find a little company for the night, everyone else having turned in.

"OK then Sidney Tombs, you convinced me." I take off my ever present apron and hang it on the hook.

Taking Sid's outstretched hand we walk down the hall and straight to bed, ready for tomorrow's chaos.

Chapter 11

Lovely

Little snuffling sounds wake me up, not that I was sleeping heavily. Glancing at the clock on the bedside in the DRMC room I'm staying in tonight, I notice that not only is it early enough to feed Bee, but it's also early enough to sneak out and put my presents under the tree for everyone to unwrap later this morning.

Rolling over, I get up, sitting on the edge of the bed and I lean into my daughter's pack and play, her dark eyes shining brightly at me in the dim light.

"Hello sweetie, Merry Christmas!" I coo at Bee, collecting her up in my arms and giving her a cuddle. I can't help but smile into her soft, dark hair, reveling in the miracle we're living.

I've never had an actual Christmas before. At the Keep the way it was spoken about and celebrated was more subdued. We celebrated Jesus' sacrifice. Here, we celebrate family and I'm all for it, as Blanche would say. I jostle Bee slightly, getting her into position, her searching mouth looking for breakfast. I place her on my breast and lean back against the headboard, thinking through the journey it's taken to get us here. Most people would think I was silly, talking about Christmas miracles all the time, but in the Keep there wasn't a lot to believe in, other than what we were told. Although that was less belief and more brainwashing I guess.

"We're going to have the best Christmas ever, little Bee. There will be smiles and gifts and lots and lots of food. There will be so much love and laughter that we won't know what to do with ourselves, it'll be just like the movies!"

She stares up at me, one hand patting my breast, her little fingers opening and closing, as if grasping at me. Looking at her, all I see is me and my sister. And our siblings. Landry genes are strong. She's a pure little soul and I cannot wait to spend many Christmases with her. She pulls away from me, obviously full, so I burp and change her, placing her in the middle of the bed so I can throw on some clothes. In the Keep I wore a lot of brown dresses. Now that I'm out I'm not sure what I should be wearing. I went shopping with my brothers after mine and Bee's escape, and went for things that I thought people wore on the outside. Jeans and Tshirts, and sometimes an oversized jumper. My brothers and I thought it looked good, but since I've been hanging out with the Ol Ladies I've decided I want to look a little cooler. I'm going to ask them to come shopping with me in the new year I think.

Putting on one of Vic's flannel shirts, I put on the baby front pack, place Bee in, and go to where I've hidden all my gifts.

"Come on Bee, we better put these out before everyone wakes up."

We, well, I, tiptoe down the dark hall, making my way to the huge Christmas tree, glowing brightly in the corner.

"What are you doing?" Chewy's slightly monotone voice asks,

giving me one heck of a fright.

"Chewy! What are you doing?"

"I asked you first."

I squint in the darkness to try and find her. Movement near the kitchen hatch catches my eye. "Oh, I see you now. I'm just delivering my presents before everyone gets up. Are you doing the same?"

"Maybe," she answers enigmatically.

"OK then."

"What the hell are you two doing up at this time?" A gruff voice asks, me and Chewy whirling around to look at the mouth of the hall.

"What are you doing?" I'm not quite sure yet who it is, I think it's either Tank, or Judge. Both have deep voices.

"I'm guessing the same as you," Judge steps into the light of the tree, holding up an armful of wrapped boxes.

"Whoa, that's really nice wrapping."

"Oh, the lady at the store did it," I'm sure he's blushing at that.

"Well, I'm going to just put the last of mine here and head back to bed," I quickly place the last of my gifts, mixing them into the ones already under the tree, not wanting anyone to see mine just yet. "There. I'll see you both in a few hours. Oh, and Merry Christmas!" I say softly before padding down the hall.

"Why the fuck are you all up? You're meant to be asleep!" I hear Switch ask loudly, and I can't help the laugh that escapes me.

"Oh Bee, this family of ours is crazy and I love it!"

Rhodie

"It's Christmas everybody! Wake up! Santa came and he found me! He found me and Cove and Elio and Niko and Bee and Rose and Junior and all the grown ups! It's Christmas! Merry Christmas!"

This is the exact reason that I fucked the life outta my girl last night nice and early. I knew that at least one of the kids would be up at the ass crack of dawn and I don't blame them. I remember waking the whole clubhouse at Christmas when I was their age.

I kiss Chewy good morning, smiling at her grumbles. She rolls over and I know it won't be long before she realizes what day it is. She makes a quick inhale and her eyes fly open "It's Christmas Rhodie!" She bounces up out of bed, hair flying everywhere.

I admire her heart shaped ass as she rummages around, grabbing her gator onesie I gifted her last night as an early Christmas present. Not that she wore it for long before she was naked under me and it was on the floor beside us.

"Merry Christmas Chomper," She coos at her pet. I wasn't that keen on keeping a gator, but given his disabilities, he's actually more like a fat, lazy dog. He spends most of his time carried around by us, or in his pen sleeping. "Hurry up babe! We have gifts to open! I can't wait to see everyone's faces when they see what we made them," she beams, strapping on the baby carrier. She's dressed as a gator with a baby gator strapped to her and it's fucking adorable as hell.

I pull on my jeans and tshirt with my cut over top and open the door for her and Chomper. She leads the way into the common room where everyone is starting to gather in various different states of undress. Fox, Nitro and Jules looking like they've just rolled in.

"Aunt Chewy! Uncle Rhodie! Merry Christmas!" Jovie sing songs, throwing her little arms around my waist, squeezing tight.

"Merry Christmas, munchkin. I can't believe all these gifts are for me!" I exclaim. Jovie throws her head back and laughs.

'No silly, they're for everyone! I saw one for Uncle Marx in there and some for Bee and some for Mama Debs and you and everyone!" She spins and dances around in her dinosaur PJ's, wiggling her butt where the tail is attached. Cove comes running into the room and they both squeal at each other, reaching a pitch so high I think only dogs can hear them.

"You know, watching their excitement kinda makes Christmas way more exciting," Rider says, carrying a cup of coffee and plopping down on the couch. "Usually we wake up at noon and eat Chinese takeout. This year we have all this to look forward to," he gestures to the tree where the three littles are on their knees pointing out whose gifts are whose. Well, the girls are. Elio is putting them in tidy piles, presumably depending on who they belong to.

"Merry Christmas everyone! Merry Christmas my babies!" Mama Debs lights up the room as she greets everyone. She kisses the kids on the head, even the older sleepy looking teens. She then kisses all the brothers on the cheek and pulls them in for hugs wishing them all a Merry Christmas. I wait for my turn and I soak it up. I haven't had a mom in a long time, but Debs fills that space, not just for me either. I mean, sure my dad, Mad Dog has his girlfriend, but Molly isn't quite the motherly type. Or really the family type. Hence why they're living it up in Hawaii for Christmas this year.

Chewy makes a beeline for the Ol Ladies so I take a seat on the couch next to Rider, shoving his leg out of the way, making sure to be rough enough that he sloshes coffee on his cut.

"Fucker," he grumbles before shoving me back.

"Merry Christmas Uncle Rhodie! Merry Christmas Uncle Rider!" Cove yells in our faces before thrusting party hats at us.

We take the flimsy paper things and … just sit there with them.

"I'm not leaving til you put them on," she says, hands slowly raising to her hips as she stares us down.

Rider and I share a look before I paste on a smile and stick the paper hat on. Hopefully it won't mess up my hair. Cove claps her hands and then whizzes off to find a new victim.

"She's going to rule us all one day," Rider mutters, making sure his hat is on securely.

"I think they all are. Even Elio. Dude may be quiet but I think that's because he's busy plotting."

"OK, it's present time!" Jovie yells fist pumping the air.

The rest of the adults all make their way to the couches and chairs, anyone missing out on a soft seat taking up positions on the floor. It's a full house, what with the dozen or so of us DRMC, the whole Tombs family, Wire's mom and the Landry brothers. Its crazy how we went from an MC of 9 to this big almost overnight

The kids work like a well oiled machine, handing out gifts to the appropriate people, which is easy enough seeing as Elio has already sorted through them all.

"OK kids, how do we want to do this?" Marx asks, knowing full well that the littles have a plan.

"I say we all open one each so everyone can ooh ahh over them and then we move to the next person. It won't take too long cos you growed ups didn't get too many presents," Jovie nods matter of factly.

Marx's lips twitch a moment before the big man yells "You heard her, one at a time and we all oohh ahh. Let's do this!"

Everything starts out reasonably tame. The brothers get guns and ammo from Mama Debs and the Ol Ladies who banded together to do the shopping for us this year. We also get some cool bandanas, butterfly knives and an assortment of video games. I mean, yeah we're grown ass men, but we like all the fun shit too. The kids get way too many Nerf guns and Blanche gets new weapons, courtesy of her Ol Man. The ex-pregnant ladies are gifted pamper packs, full of whatever stuff goes in one of those. Lovely's eyes well up when she unwraps it and it's then, in her wobbly voice she explains that this is her first proper Christmas. Well, shit. If we had known that I'm sure the brothers would have gone all out. She's much like Remy, a total sweetheart. I'm also fairly certain Marx likes her. As in likes her likes her, but he's a stubborn bastard so I'm sure it'll take a fucking miracle to get these two on the same page.

"Chewy you didn't!" Blanche gasps and our attention swings in Elio's direction, who is standing with a huge box, the picture on the front is a kid in a lab coat. "My First Chemistry Lab" emblazoned in massive letters.

"What? I took the black powder out," Dayz says defensively.

"Wait, isn't that gun powder?" Tank asks, Judge nodding in confirmation.

"He'll be fully supervised by me and Pops."

"That's what I'm afraid of," Marx answers drily before giving Elio a smile and thumbs up, not wanting to ruin Elio's obvious excitement.

"What the fuck?" Nitro grumbles, looking perplexed as he pulls a dildo out of the box he's just opened, holding it by the knob. He pulls and we all see that there is a chain attached to the taint of the dildo.

"What the hell is this?" Fox asks. He too is holding a knob, but he's holding his up high in the air so we can all see that the chain is not only attached to the dildo in his hand, but also another dildo on the other end.

"Merry Christmas! They're dongchucks!" Dayz yells. "You know, like nunchucks, but with dongs! Also, they're super heavy so they're bound to do a lot of damage."

All the brothers move to their gifts, rummaging around until they are all holding dongchucks up in the air.

"Well, that's one way to get rid of them," Nat whispers to Ana and Remy, the two of them cackling, while Blanche wrestles Tav's out of his hand so she can give them a go.

"Score! Even we got some!" One of the Landry's yells out. I'm not sure which one, they all look the same.

"While we're on the dildos, Jules, would you like to open your gift?" Chewy says, her cheeks pink with excitement.

"Yeah Uncle Jules, open it! Open it" The kids then start chanting to perhaps the grumpiest of all the grown ups.

Jules complies, carefully unwrapping the gator decorated paper, revealing two dildos. One has a blonde mullet with a red bandanna over the top, a yellow vest, and the balls have been painted red. The other one has a brown mullet, tiger print bandanna, and tiger and leopard print on the shaft and balls.

He stares at it for a moment before throwing his head back and laughing, a rumble shaking his whole body.

"Holy shit, I've never seen him do that," Ana says, wide eyed.

"Wait, are those dicks dressed like Hulk Hogan and Macho Man Randy Savage?" Dex asks incredulously.

"Holy shit! They are too!" Tav yells, pointing while the brothers burst into laughter.

"He always wanted the dolls when we were kids and never got them," Dayz says seriously.

"Well, shit. Now he does," Pops cackles, leaning on a laughing Debs who's rocking one of the babies in her arms. It's dressed in blue so I'm guessing it's Junior Pops.

"Those things are badass and insane in equal measure," Switch loudly points out.

I smile to myself and wait for my Ol Lady to give me the signal.

"Babe, would you please bring in the clubhouse gift?"

"As you wish, baby."

I head out of the common room and into one of the spare rooms Chewy commandeered for "Christmas Crafts". I really need to get her someone to torture because I cannot take another trip to Hobby Lobby. No way. Gathering up our surprise gift I laugh to myself. Shit I can't wait for the brothers to see this. We were clever enough to mount this thing on wheels so I wheel it into the common room.

"Is that a wrestling ring?" someone asks.

"Yup! Elio, would you and the littles please hand out the boxes with gators on them please?"

The kids nod, then race around delivering the gift boxes.

The brothers dig in, each box that is opened is met with raucous laughter. Chewy in her spare time, has made dildo wrestlers for each and every brother. The Rock, The Undertaker, Batista, Stone Cold, and pretty much any title holding wrestler you can think of. Between them and the dongchucks I think she may have finally exhausted her supply of rubber dicks.

The brothers all pull my Ol Lady in for a hug, making sure not to squash Chomper, wishing her Merry Christmas and she beams, her face lit up from within. I catch her gaze and she gives me two thumbs up.

"See Rhodie! I told you the Cricut was worth it!"

Chewy

I take it all in. The way the room seems to burst with laughter. This is my family and I love them. Even if they did do a little too much hugging.

"Nice job, girl."

"Thank you Pops. I just had to think about what wrestler each person would like. Or what each kid would like. It was fun trying to get into their heads."

"I'm proud of you. Look how far you've come, kiddo. You have an Ol Man that I don't want to kill. You have all these friends,"

"Family, Pops."

He nods at me, "Yup. Family. You even have a gator baby." He rubs his hand down Chomper's body, and then gives me a smile.

"Well, after those awesome gifts, it seems right to give Dayz hers," Mama Debs says.

I don't know what it could be. I haven't really told anyone what I wanted for my first DRMC Christmas, mainly because I already had everything I wanted. Having a surprise gifted to me means that I have to remember to look and act excited and appreciative so people won't think I hate it. Even if I do. It's the thought that counts.

Mama Debs and the Ol Ladies all leave the room, then come back pushing a stroller. But it's not any stroller, it's been pimped! The ergonomic stroller has had the main part where the baby hangs out elongated some, long enough to accommodate a tail. There's fun toys clipped to the shade cover, good thick silicone ones that Chomper will be able to snap at, and maybe even gnaw a little. His jaw is quite weak because of his severe underbite, but he does like to try to bite things. Maybe these chewies will help strengthen things? But that's not all. The whole thing has been reupholstered in a nice green, with a gator pattern running through it. It even has cup holders AND like a skateboard thing at the back so I can use it like a push scooter.

My eyes are darting everywhere trying to take it all in. "It's beautiful," I croak out. There is something wrong in my throat, it feels tight but not in a bad way. "Rhodie, did you see it? It, it's wonderful."

My eyes are feeling wet and I have to blink to try and stop them from welling up. I'm not sure what's wrong but it just feels... odd. I was prepared to do my good acting because I thought it would be something nice, but something that I wasn't particularly interested in or needed. But this is the opposite. It's thoughtful and everyone put effort into it because it's something they knew I would love. They did this for me.

A warm weight presses up against my leg, and I look down at the top of a dark head.

"The feeling is big, Chewy?"

I nod, then realize I have to use words. "The feeling is very big, Elio."

"That's what it feels like all the time here. It's big in a good way." He pats my knee then heads back to his boxed up lab, rubbing his hand over the picture.

"Come on baby, let's test her out, huh?" Rhodie's scent wraps around me as he takes his big warm hands, and presses down on my shoulders, the pressure bringing me back into myself a little.

"Yes, let's do it!" I start unbuckling Chomper from his front pack, then maneuver him into his new ride. He settles into the soft mattress with a little sigh, before relaxing and promptly going to sleep.

"It's a hit!" Rhodie yells, fists in the air. Everyone starts cheering and I push Chomper around the room, saying thank you first to my girl gang, and then to all the brothers.

Everyone deserves my thanks. Not only did these people befriend me, the weird kid, but they also put up with my gator and then gifted me the best Christmas gift ever!

"OK, we have more gifts! Open these ones next," Jovie bosses, her and her little minions dropping little wrapped packages in all the brothers laps.

"I wonder what the kids have made," Blanche ponders.

"They have been spending a lot of time in Jovie's tent, scheming," Remy answers.

The guys start opening the little gifts, all while the kids watch with rapt attention.

"Hey, it's a guardian bell!" Flack says, jingling the little bell in the air.

"A bell? What for?" Ana asks the room, looking perplexed.

"It's a guardian bell, Aunt Ana. You gotta put it on your bike and it'll protect you from bad stuff," Jovie answers matter of factly.

"That's exactly right. And you can't buy one yourself, it has to be gifted to you," Flack says, before scooping Jovie up for a hug.

"It's to protect you grandpa. And all my uncles," she says. "It was Elio's idea. He wanted everyone to be safe."

I flick my gaze to Elio who is looking very interested in

anything that isn't all the big men looking at him. I push Chomper closer to him, and then take a seat, my leg touching his.

"Big," I whisper down to him.

"Big," he whispers in return.

"Thank you kids, this is awesome. I'm going to put mine on my bike right now," Marx says, then leaves the room, all the brothers thanking the kids and leaving the room.

"Aw kids, that is so sweet of you," Remy says. Nat and Ana wipe away tears. They do that a lot now.

"I'd love to know how you three littles went shopping without any of us knowing about it," Blanche asks, her dark brow raised extra scary like.

"Don't worry mom, I was with them. So was Takoda. They were safe the whole time," Niko answers. Blanche squints at him and then nods slowly.

The brothers all file back in, taking their places again.

"We are onto the last of the presents," Cove announces, "and they're the ones from Santa!" she adds extra loud in case people in the next town didn't hear her.

They all get passed around and I brace myself to most definitely find something that I will have to pretend to like. Taking the wrapping off carefully I find a Mr Creepy Magic kit.

"No way," I breathe out. I wanted one of these so bad when I was a kid, but after one too many failed magic shows in front of my parents, they kinda gave up trying to encourage me. In all fairness the main issue was that Tav was my beautiful assistant and he was bad at following directions.

There's whooping and laughter from the rest of the room, and more than one person exclaiming that it's something they always wanted when they were a kid.

"Mama Debs! Was this you and the Ol Ladies?" Sniper asks.

Debs holds up her hands, "It wasn't us. We bought you guns and stuff."

Hmmm. Interesting. I stroke my imaginary beard, seems like someone pulled a Secret Santa.

"Look babe! I can make us cookies in bed!" Rhodie says, holding up his Easy Bake oven, snapping me out of my pondering.

I hold up my magic kit, "And I can saw a man in half!" I reply across the room to him.

"You do that anyway, Chewy!" Someone yells out and I have to laugh. I mean, he's not wrong there.

The gifts are all open and the big kids start clearing up the trash. The babies are being fed, Rhodie has ripped open his oven, Elio is wearing his safety goggles, Cove is making something out of Playdoh, the teenagers are on their new phones, one half of the brothers are playing with their dongchucks, the other half are playing with their dildo wrestlers in the ring my Ol Man made. And holy crap is that a dog? Jovie starts wailing, her parents hugging her, introducing her to the largest puppy I've ever seen. The Landrys stare and I get it. These guys came from a cult and now they're here. With all these people enjoying a nice, normal Christmas.

"You know, I should find this weird, and yet I really don't," Chris says to me, Dom nodding in agreement.

"I think we've been brainwashed somehow," Vic adds.

"It happens." Marx says, coming to stand with us. "Not long ago I had an MC that was small and well disciplined. Then we met the Tombs' and now we're this big weird family and watching guys use dildos as ninja weapons seems completely run of the mill."

"Would you have it any other way?" Vic asks, brow raised.

"Fuck no," Marx replies, sending a wink in my direction.
I agree. I wouldn't have it any other way either.

Chapter 12

Blanche

I finish wiping the last bench and decide now would be the perfect time to sneak off. "I'm off Mama Debs, thank you so much for breakfast," I whisper in her ear, giving her shoulder a squeeze. After we unwrapped all the gifts Debs went straight into breakfast mode, bossing the three prospects around like she was Gordon Ramsey.

"Anytime, dear. Now why don't you go have a nap while I keep Tav busy helping me out here." She gives me a wink and I grin back.

Taking a quick look around I make sure no one will notice me. Not that they would. Sage is helping out here in the kitchen, which very handily puts her in Takoda's orbit. I see her giving him moony eyes. She notices me, rolling hers when she sees my wide-eyed stare and raised brows. I raise my hand, pointing my fingers at my eyes, then at her, then back to me. The little sass pot just grins at me and goes back to chatting with Takoda.

"She'll be fine, momma," Debs says, then hip bumps me toward the door.

I know Sage will be fine. She takes after me, of course. Not to mention Niko has her back, as dos Tav and the rest of the men around here. It's just that, she's my baby. My little girl. No matter how old she gets she always will be. So will the others. They're all my babies. My chest starts feeling a little tight and my lip starts to wobble. Then my head starts pounding and I can hear my heartbeat in my ears. Oh hell no. No, no way. I've been extra tired lately and a little moody. Maybe it's perimenopause? You get all teary and emotional with perimenopause don't you? Shit.

I check the Littles, seeing they're busy playing with their new toys with the MC brothers, then I hightail it into Tav's room, kicking the door shut and diving into the luxurious pillows Tav has piled up high. Even though we had a late night last night, and then got up early thanks to the Littles demanding we get up, he still made the bed and piled them high. So I can cry into them.

Shit, shit shit. I need reinforcements. Wrestling my phone out of my sweatpants, because who the hell wears real pants on Christmas Day, I send a panic text to my girl gang and anxiously wait. Which is about 30 seconds before I hear the pattering of feet coming down the hall.

Bang! "Whoops, sorry Chomper!" sounds out on the other side of the door before it's kicked in, Chewy's hair and eyes wild.

"What's the SOS? Has someone been kidnapped? Someone know sensitive information that you need extracted? A rescue perhaps?"

I stare at her as she looks around the room as if I've hidden a hostage or something. Damn, Tav's right. She really does need to cut something or someone up. "Um, no, none of those things."

"Ok, we're here! The babies are both down, their dads are on watch and we came as quickly as our stitches would allow," Ana announces, her and Nat high fiving each other as they shuffle into the room and take a seat on the bed.

"Damn, this place is niiiiice!" Nat says, looking around. "Tav must have done all this, I've seen your place."

"Hey! What's wrong with my place?"

"Nothing. It's just a lived-in family home, full of memories and cushions that don't match." She shrugs, smiling up at Remy and Lovely as the two nicest members of the gang walk in. Remy raises her brows at me indicating the door and I nod, watching as she closes it gently.

"OK, Blanche, what's with the SOS?" Nat asks, sinking into the cushions next to me.

I take a deep breath and then let it out slowly. Before I can open my mouth the door opens and my brothers come running in, giggling like little girls. They shut the door, turn and freeze as the girl gang stares back at them.

"Can we help you, gentlemen?" I ask, squinting at Vic, Chris and Dom. When they don't answer I raise my brow ever so slowly, then glare. I have shit to talk through with my girls and I can't do that with those three in here. They'll blab.

Vic tilts his head, brows pinching as he stares at me. His eyes widen and they dart toward Dom and Chris as they shrink back into the closed door.

"What are they doing? Why do they look like that?" Chewy asks, staring at the three idiots who are trying to open the door without breaking eye contact with me. As if I'm going to jump off the bed and eat them alive.

"They know something they shouldn't know," Ana says, amusement in her voice.

"Really?" Chewy replies, a little too excited. "Tell me your secrets gator men," she says menacingly, taking a step toward them.

They look at each other, then back to Chewy. "She's pregnant!" One or all of them yell before Vic gets the door open and they flee.

Five sets of eyes all turn back to me. Four of them wide, one of them narrowed.

"Wait, how old are you? Aren't you older than Tav? That would definitely put you in the geriatric pregnancy category," Chewy announces at the same time Lovely starts to tear up and whisper about Christmas miracles.

Remy is beaming at me, her hands silently clapping at the news while Ana grimaces and crosses her legs a little.

I turn my gaze to Nat. "I should have just called you."

She grins at that and then claps her hands, getting everyone's attention. "Who of you has a pregnancy test in their room?"

It's dead silent, then Remy slowly raises her hand. "We've not been trying, but we've not not been trying either. I have a couple in my room. Wait right here."

She scuttles off down the hall and I can feel my anxiety rising every second that she's away.

"Tav is a good dad. He loves kids and he will love any more you have," Chewy says in all seriousness. "You will need to have extra tests and visits to monitor the health of the fetus, what with you being old and all."

Ana snorts so hard that she gives herself a coughing fit and I don't have any sympathy for her.

"Here is it! Go in there and pee sister!" Remy tosses the test on the bed and I stare at it like it's going to bite me.

"You can do this Blanche. You're an amazing mother," Lovely

coos, smiling gently at me and she rocks Bee back and forth in her front pack.

"You're right. I'm a fucking badass. I raised four kids on my own. I can raise four kids and a baby. I'm not alone, I have the best man I've ever met who loves me and will support me. Let's do this!" I snatch up the test in my fist, raise it high and let out a battle cry.

"Um, what's happening?"

Tav

I stare at the six members of the girl gang as they whoop and holler, led by my Ol Lady who is standing on the bed, a white stick held high in her fist as she makes that Xena war cry sound.

"A Christmas miracle," Lovely whispers, then pecks me on the cheek on her way out, the other women slowly following behind her. Well, all bar Chewy who is standing in the room looking from my Pixie, to me and then back again.

"Oh, I guess I better leave too." She shrugs, then does a 73 point turn, trying to maneuver Chomper's stroller out of the small space.

Pixie and I watch with rapt fascination as she finally manages to get out the door, then slamming it behind her.

"So, that was weird, right?"

Blanche looks down at me from her place on the bed, and nods. Her dark eyes are huge and she looks pale.

"Pixie, are you OK? Did you eat something weird?"

She holds her hand out to me and I take a good look. It's a

little stick thing and I have no clue what it is until I notice the open box on the bed, the picture on the front a smiley, pregnant woman.

"Pixie?" My voice comes out hoarse, and I clench my fists to stop my hands from shaking. I'm not sure if the swirling in my gut is excitement or fear. I mean, I'm already a father. I have four kids out in the common room, each of them filling my heart with equal amounts of love and fear. But a baby? A baby I made with my Ol Lady? They're tiny and helpless and holy shit what if I ruin them!

"Tav! Babe, sit down!" Pixie launches herself at me and I can't not catch her in my arms. Her weight brings me to my knees on the bed and she bodily moves me until we're lying on my cushion collection. "Are you OK? I mean, I may not be pregnant. I could have perimenopause," she says, trying to soothe me.

I roll my head to the side to look at her, my beautiful Pixie. "Babe, we've been slack with condoms and it's been weeks since I remember your last shark week."

"Yeah," she sighs. "Do you, do you think you'll be happy if it's positive?" Her brow pinches and she looks up at me worriedly.

"Patience Blanche Landry. I love you. With everything in me. Having a family with you is more than I had ever dreamed of. Whether it's just the four out there, or whether it's our four out there and one in here," I rest my palm on her soft belly, "I would be honored to do life, this life with you."

She stares at me, as if trying to find the lie, but she will never find one. I was made to be the father of her children. "I love you Tav." She presses her lips to mine in a sweet kiss. "I'm going to pee."

"And I'll hold your hand."

"Ah, I'm gonna need you not to, dude. Maybe just stand outside the door and don't listen, yeah?"

"Fine. But we're gonna have to pop that 'pee in front of each other' cherry sooner or later."

She screws up her face as she walks into the bathroom, leaving the door slightly ajar. "We'll never be that couple. I want to keep a little mystery between us."

"How can you when I'll be down the business end helping birth my baby?"

"No way Octavius Tombs!" she splutters.

I smile to myself as my little plan worked. My woman is much better working through big emotions and ideas when she's a little irritated. And I feel like her working through the thought of being pregnant is a big thing to work through.

There's some rustling on the other side of the door, then the flushing of the toilet and running water.

"OK. It's done. We will know our fate in 3 minutes. Distract me."

"Three minutes you say?" I waggle my brows at her as I pull her into my arms.

We have three minutes on the pregnancy test clock, and I have about ten minutes before I'm needed back in the kitchen for the dinner service. Plenty of time to relax my woman. Pulling her into my arms, I run my hands down her back, gripping her luscious ass before working my way back up, all the way to the nape of her neck, squeezing a little then moving up a little further and cupping the back of her head as I lean forward and devour her plump pink lips.

She moans into the kiss, giving me access to taste her. I move her head slightly, deepening the kiss and tugging on her short dark strands, mussing up her cute little pixie cut.

"Tav, please, I need you now." Her hands move to rub my hard length, the denim not thick enough to stop the heat of her hand branding my cock as hers, hers alone.

Dropping to my knees I yank her sweatpants and panties down in one smooth movement, not even waiting for her to step out of them. I lean into her and flick her clit with my tongue, gripping her thick thighs I move her to where I need her to be - making love to my mouth.

"Ah, shit, yes, fuck Tav, your tongue, holy shit." She's panting and riding my tongue, chasing her pleasure and there is nowhere I'd rather be than on my knees lapping at her sweet pussy.

Giving her thighs a little squeeze I release them, one hand moving up to circle her tight hole, the other moving above, stroking through the fine hairs on her mound to find that little button that makes her go wild. Applying pressure to her clit I take her plump lower lips into my mouth and suck gently as I curl my fingers and tap at the rough patch inside her.

"Tav!" Her hands fly to the top of my head, gripping on for dear life as she bucks wildly, her legs shaking as the pressure of her release erupts. I look up the length of her body and I'm fucking awe struck. My Pixie is stunningly beautiful as she relishes in her pleasure.

I drink the last of her sweet cream, then gather her in my arms as the last of the aftershocks jolt through her, her legs no longer able to hold her up. I expect her to snuggle into my arms, fully sated and ready for a nap, but I'm mistaken.

Quick as a flash she has my zipper open and my cock poking through the gaping denim, her mouth on me in such hunger that I let out a high pitched yelp. I would be embarrassed but my eyes have rolled into the back of my head and all my nerve endings are on fire as she sucks the soul right out of my dick.

"Fuck, baby, that mouth! Holy shit, I'm not going to last," I gasp, my hips thrusting into her hot wet mouth without my say so. That's how far gone I am for this woman. Seeing those thick pink lips wrapped around the mushroom head of my throbbing cock undoes me.

I cup her face, trying to move her off so I don't come in her mouth, but Pixie has other ideas. Taking me to the back of her throat and swallowing as I unload into her hot little mouth with a long, low groan. I fall back on my ass, my head lolling on my shoulders. Then I hear the unmistakable sound of gagging. I should know that sound, Rider makes it all the time.

"Fuck, Pixie, are you OK sweetheart?" I blink the post orgasmic haze out of my eyes just in time to see her make a dash to the toilet and throw up.

I follow her, ignoring my softening manhood hanging out the front of my jeans and rub her back.

"Ugh, sorry babe, that wasn't quite the finish I was going for," she says, slumping down onto the floor.

"I tried to move you off but you were like a dog with a bone," I say, chuckling when she replies "Boner."

"Help me up and we can rinse our mouths, don't want pussy and cock breath for Christmas," she grins up at me.

We gently tussle, trying to get to the basin first before we both clock the test on the sink and freeze.

"Is that?"

"Yup. Two lines."

"That means?" I gulp, my stomach fizzing with love and fear and excitement and I feel like on Christmas morning.

"Merry Christmas, Tav."

Chapter 13

Pops

Marx bangs his fist on the long table, signaling he has something to say. We've just finished with the dessert course and I am full as a bull. I'm fucking glad I don't have to sing and dance anytime soon because I have the meat sweats and there's no room in my pants for any hip thrusts.

"I just wanted to quickly say Merry Christmas DRMC!" Marx yells, raising his beer bottle to cheers from around the table. "This year is the first year in a long time that we've sat down to a real, home-cooked Christmas meal. Thank you, Mama Debs, for looking after us like we're your sons. We appreciate you and everything you do for us."

I bang the table a few times as the brothers all clap and cheer for her. Debs is blushing and waving her hand at them, trying to get them to stop but I'm not having it. Leaning forward I whisper in her ear. "You deserve it, sweetheart." She beams up at me and I grin back. She's worth all the praise and more.

"Don't think I've forgotten the rest of you ladies. You all

stepped up majorly, helping with the toy drive and backing up Mama Debs in the kitchen with the Christmas meals and tonight's menu. Thank you, Remy, Nat, Ana, Lovely, Blanche, Debs and yes, you too Chewy." Snickers are heard around the table as Dayz's head pops up from where she's been concentrating on hand feeding Chomper bits of turkey. "I used to think that the DRMC was a bunch of retired brothers in arms who came home and built not only an MC, but a family. But I was wrong. You Ol Ladies, having your loyalty, kindness and your support is what made us a family."

"The one million kids that joined us didn't hurt, either!" Switch yells, the table all laughing at his comment.

I mean, there are a shit ton of kids in a very short time. If I'm right about what I'm seeing across the table from me, Tav and Blanche grinning like fools and whispering to each other, I'm sure the number of kids in the compound is going to rise.

"So, thank you everyone for making this Christmas fucking awesome!" Everyone claps, Blanche puts two fingers in her mouth and lets out an ear piercing whistle and all the brothers hoot and holler and make almost as much noise as Cove did this morning opening her presents.

I throw my arm around Debs and pull her in close. "Merry Christmas, love." I whisper, then kiss her on the temple.

She turns her big brown eyes on me searching my face for something, I'm not sure what. She must see what she's looking for because a smile spreads across her face as she leans in, and presses her lips gently to mine before pulling back and repeating my words. "Merry Christmas, love."

I gaze around the table, my eyes meeting Rider's. He narrows his eyes then gives me a single nod. It's about to be game on.

"Come on, ladies and Littles, let's retire to the couches and let these guys start on clearing the table, yeah?" I say loudly. The MC brothers all nod at my cue, pushing their chairs back and getting to work.

Even the Bigs are eager to join in, as are Gus and Jules knowing full well what's about to happen. In any normal circumstances a group of men cleaning the dining room and kitchen would drag, and fights would break out. Not tonight, tonight is all about Debs. I give Dayz the signal and she gives me a salute, shoulder tapping Elio to follow her. It's important in pyrotechnics to run your checks one last time before showtime. There is no room for any mistakes tonight. I want this to be perfect for Debs. I want her to know how special she is to me. No matter how much time we have together, the risk is worth the reward.

Within half an hour the bloat has started to subside and the room is sparkling clean, put back to rights. "Babe, would you mind getting your coat on and coming outside for a walk with me?"

Debs gives me a funny look. I can tell she's suspicious. I would be too. The poor woman probably thinks I'm love bombing her. She squints at me a moment, then flicks her gaze to Ana who is grinning and giving her the thumbs up. "Ok, Sid. What are you up to?"

"Nothing," I reply as innocently as I can. I'm not sure she completely believes the innocent act, but she gets up anyway and wanders to her room to find her coat. As soon as she's out of ear shot I spin around to address the MC. "It's showtime you fuckers, don't let me down!"

"Yeah, yeah. I told you already you silly old fart, we've got this." Rider says, rolling his eyes. Marx is trying hard not to laugh, the bastard.

"Half of you head out there now, the rest of you follow behind me and Debs. *At a distance.* We don't want her to be suspicious."

"They've got this, Pops." Marx's giant hand lands on my shoulder, and he indicates the box with her cut in it that I've been keeping in his office since I had a close call with her finding it earlier in the week. "Remember, if you hurt her, we hurt you." He winks at me but I feel the threat down to my toes. And then I shake it off because we all know I'm scarier than these young bucks.

Half of the MC skedaddle outside just as Debs' footsteps can be heard coming back down the hall. I know they have costumes that the Ol Ladies helped them with, they're all being kept in the gym so I need to buy a little time for the first men out to suit up. Then buy more time once we're in place for the second group of men to suit up. Holy shit this surprise is a logistical nightmare, but it'll all be worth it in the end to see her face.

"Ready my dear?" I hold my elbow out and Debs takes it, still studying my face to find out why the hell I'm acting weird. Or normal. Because I guess this is normal romantic courting. I think. I'll have to ask someone who isn't related to me.

"You're up to something. I can tell. You're all squirrely."

"Nah, it's just the Christmas spirit. Are you kids and ladies coming for a walk? Get rid of some of that energy?" I ask the Littlies who all jump up and busy themselves putting on coats. And then trying to find their shoes. Lovely helps them look, little Bee fast asleep in her front pack. Chewy is putting a hat on Chomper and Ana and Nat are making sure their babies are snug as bugs in rugs. "Ready?" They all nod and we set off.

Thankfully the kids decide to piss around in the parking lot, wanting to know which bike Debs thinks is the prettiest. The consensus is that Remy's bike is the prettiest, what with her having a new paint job. The bike she acquired after Snake's timely demise has been given a new lick of paint. Not pink for our Remy. Her's sports a hard candy purple paint job that Cove and Jovie like to oooh and ahh over.

"I wonder if Remy will take me for a spin?" Debs muses.

I shut that down real quick. "If you want a ride you ride with me, no one else. Got it?"

She stares at me for a moment then rolls her eyes. "Alright cave man. Your bike it is. When are you gonna take me for a whirl?" she asks, patting my chest.

"Whenever you like, babe. But first, I want to show you something, it's just around the corner."

I wrap my large leathery hand around her small soft one and tug her toward the back. The kids dance either side of us as we're met with Marx, Gus, Jules, and the Landrys standing in front of a makeshift stage.

"Sidney, what's going on?" Debs looks around wildly as I lead her to one of the Game of Dong's throne's that were set up for the baby showers a couple of months back.

"Take a seat and all will be revealed."

She sits in the throne, the other women sitting in outdoor chairs around her. We wait a moment and nothing happens.

"I said, take a seat and all will be revealed!" I say, louder this time. Come on fuckers, that's you're cue. Nothing happens again and I'm starting to look like I've lost my marbles. "ALL WILL BE REVEA-OH!"

Debs

Pops' shout is interrupted by the twanging of a guitar. The stage that is sitting in the backyard is a little dark, and I can't quite see who it is that steps up clearly but I think it might be Switch.

"This is going out to a special woman," he starts off, the voices of the other brothers making deep "oooohhhh" sounds as he continues. "A kind woman, a proud woman!"

The lights go up and Switch is center stage in tight black shorts and a leather jacket with sequins and tassels. No shirt underneath, his red chest hair out for all to see.

"*Aue!* What in the heck is going on?" I stare wide eyed at the vision in front of me.

Switch brings the microphone up to his mouth and in a smooth, rich voice he starts to sing.

"*Left a good job in New Zealand, working for the man every night and day-*"

Takoda's impossibly deep voice blends in with him and it's then that I notice the MC all dressed the same as Switch making shoop shoop motions behind him.

"*And she never lost one minute of sleepin'-*" They all twirl in synchronicity, and I must say the choreography is well done. For a bunch of men that I would never have thought would even know how to dance.

The Ol Ladies beside me whoop and holler, Nat even has a wad of cash out and is yelling at Savage to "Shake that ass!". Dayz is in a makeshift booth with Elio so I'm guessing they're the lighting and sound crew. We hit the big wheel part and I can't help but shimmy in my seat as I join in singing with my boys.

Holy crap! Eleven male voices all harmonize perfectly and I'm blown away, so surprised that I get to my feet and clap loudly. Hooting and hollering for my boys. Switch slows it right down and I know what's coming up. It's my favorite part of this song. I hold my breath and wait for the beat and what's going to happen next. Switch doesn't disappoint as he does a high kick and the drum and trumpets blast out, Chewy and Elio's lighting show flashing to the beat of the music.

"*Oh left a good job in New Zealand,*" Switch sings again, strutting from one side of the stage to the other, giving high fives to both the Bigs and the Littles as he struts his stuff, a big, ginger replica of Tina Turner. Me and the ladies yell "Turnin" at the appropriate time at the top of our lungs, nowhere near as harmonized as the men on stage but we don't care. "*Proud Debs keep on burnin!*" I throw my head back and laugh at the change of lyrics.

I'm breathless not only from dancing, but from watching eleven big, burly men in short tight pants and tassels all pump their arms as they act out the "rolling" part of the song. They roll their arms then stomp to opposite sides of the stage to roll them once more, Switch is wiggling like his rent is due and all the men are singing at the top of their voices. It's the most magnificent sight I have ever seen in my life and I know whose idea this was.

"You did this, didn't you?" I look up at Sid, who has a look of awe on his face. Not for the men in front of us, but for me.

He cups my face and smiles softly. "You deserve this and so much more. Probably a whole concert."

I grin up at him and then turn just in time to see the boys "do do do do do" and my god, can some of these boys shake their asses! The whoops from the women are ear piercing, the kids are laughing themselves silly and I can't take my eyes off how loose Sniper and Dex's hips are.

"Good lord ladies, look at those hips!"

All seven of us women are mesmerized as we watch Sniper and Dex gyrate on the stage, Magic Mike style. Is it hot in here?

"Hey, I have hips right here for you to ogle," Sid grumbles.

"Yeah, but they don't move like that," I reply, the ladies cackling next to me.

"Holy moly, I need to get them to teach me how to do that," Lovely says in awe.

"No you don't, your hips are fine," Marx says briskly, before turning back to look at the stage, as if he didn't speak at all.

I side eye Remy who rolls her lips between her teeth, and we try not to laugh at Marx's statement. Lovely isn't bothered however, she's holding Bee's head to her chest as she wiggles what her mama gave her anyway.

The men are breathless from their non-stop thrusting and hip rolling, Switch is hitting the high notes and the 'audience' are in fits of laughter. Who knew that shiny shorts would bring this out in the men?

"Marx, I think we've just seen our next fundraiser. DRMC in Concert. Think about how much you'd raise!" Ana says.

Nat makes sounds of agreement, but not taking her eyes off her man. "It's lucky I'm out of action for a few weeks. Seeing Savage like that, all shiny and tassle-y in those tight little shorts is making my ovaries weep. Weep I tell ya!"

"Oh hell," Pops says, running a hand down his face.

"This is all your fault, Pops," Marx accuses.

The music starts to slow and all the men, at Switch's instruc-tion start circling one arm around, in an Elvis-like move as they thrust in time to the fading music before lining up, and taking a deep bow. I rush to the stage, clapping all the while and pull

Switch in for a hug.

"You were fabulous! Thank you! Thank all of you!" I work my way down the line, hugging them all one by one. First Rhodie, then Rider, Tank who's shorts are almost indecent, Judge, whose shorts are most definitely indecent, then Fox, Nitro, Flack, who is too old for his shorts. Almost. Savage, gives me a quick squeeze then hightails it to his appreciative wife, as does Wire as soon as I let him go. Loose hips Dex and Sniper get hugs, then Tav, Takoda and the other prospect, Jimmy.

"I don't deserve your time or the effort that went into this, but I very, very much appreciate it and love it with all my heart. Thank you, my boys. You made me proud," I sniffle, wiping my eyes.

They all beam at me as they step down from the stage, then turn to watch Pops climb up and come to a stop in front of me, reaching out to clasp my hands.

"Debs. I knew you were something special the moment I laid eyes on you, all fresh faced and looking for adventure. I knew I could offer you that adventure, but what I couldn't offer you was anything more than fun. We've both lost love in the past, and at my age you know that death is always breathing down your neck."

"Death can't catch the Devil, old man," Rhodie's rough voice calls, the boys sniggering. Pops answers them by holding up my middle finger, not taking his eyes off me.

"Sid, we spoke about this. No one is guaranteed a long life. Or even a tomorrow," I implore. This silly man thinks he's saving my heart by not committing. But it's too late, my heart already belongs to him.

"I know, sweetheart. I was just being old and stubborn and a fucking idiot. You are the light in a lot of people's lives, but especially mine. And the thought of you not shining that light on me everyday, me being in the dark because I was a stupid fool who lost the best thing that's happened to him, well, that's a life not worth living." My heart thuds in my chest and I feel all gooey at his words. He cups my cheeks in his large hands, gazing into my eyes. He swallows and licks his lips, "Debs, will you be my Ol lady?"

The tears that were dancing along my lash line break free and my throat is thick so I nod and throw my arms around Sid's neck, pulling him close. "Yes, yes you silly old man, I'll be your Ol Lady."

I pull back and kiss him, pouring all my feelings into the kiss. For months now I had felt I was in limbo. I love my new home and my new family. I love this man but I was starting to feel as if our relationship was a little one sided, as if I was forcing it to be more than what it was. With this surprise from Sid, the concert he forced the guys into and his declaration, well, everything feels the way it should. Settled. Perfect. Forever.

Marx steps up beside us with a large box in his hands, holding it so Sid can open it. He moves the tissue paper, grips whatever is inside and slowly pulls it out of the box, revealing a buttery leather cut with "Debs" on the front where the brothers names go, and "Property of Pops" underneath.

I look out into the crowd and see so many smiling faces as Pops slips my cut on. The weight feels just right, wrapping around me, just like Sid's arm across my shoulders.

"SHOWTIME!" Chewy yells and loud popping noises ring out just moments before the sky lights up so brightly I'm sure I'll be seeing stars for the next few hours.

"Holy shit it's like watching a nuclear bomb go off!" Nitro yells.

"Wait, does that spell out 'Suck it losers'?"

"Yes, because I have the very best Ol Lady!" Sid crows, cackling at the brothers' protests. I give him a gentle jab in the ribs, trying to hide my smile.

"Here's the best part," He says, leaning down to whisper in my ear.

The sky goes dark for a moment and then whistles and pops split the air, the sky lighting up in a brilliant pink, with the words "I love you Debs."

"I love you too."

Marx

I lean back in my office chair, the leather creaking slightly under my weight. Today was a good day. I chuckle to myself thinking over the highlights in my mind, especially Pops and his damned surprise. The guys worked hard to gift Debs something she loved and I'm fucking proud of them all. I pour myself another three fingers of whiskey and swirl it around, spinning to look at the photos on the wall. Pictures of my dad Mad Dog and the original brothers. Pictures of me and my brother in the military, group photos of the men that make up the MC and my closest friends. I didn't know what we were missing until Chewy broke into our compound and showed us that the love of a good woman lifts you up and gives you something to grasp onto with both hands. All my men who have an Ol Lady have grown in ways I would never have expected. They're better men, hell, all of us are better men for it.

"Knock, knock," a voice quietly calls out.

Spinning in my chair I'm met with Lovely's soft smile. She's gently rocking back and forth in the doorway, most likely to settle Bee, although I've noticed her doing it even if Bee isn't with her.

"Lovely, come on in." She gives me a little nod and carefully walks into the room, slowly as if something is going to jump out at her.

"You missed your gift from Santa, so I thought I would deliver it to you. Merry Christmas, Marx." She hands me a brightly wrapped box and turns to leave.

"Please, stay. Let's see what Santa brought me, huh?" I gesture to her to move closer. I offer her the chair across from me but she shakes her head, patting Bee and swaying gently. I nod in understanding.

Carefully peeling off the wrapping a laugh bursts out of me at what is revealed. "It's Mr Potato Head! I always wanted one of these as a kid. I wrote so many letters to Santa asking for Mr Potato Head, told all my family and friends and yet never got one."

"Well, now you do. Must be a Christmas miracle." She beams at me, her eyes glistening.

I stare at her, her dark hair shining in the light. "Thank you, Lovely."

"It was nothing. I was just delivering what Santa dropped off."

"Ah, yes." I say, stroking my beard. "Santa. The same Santa that snuck into the common room early this morning to put the gifts under the tree? That Santa?"

She smiles and nods. "Yup. That same one."

"Huh. I'm sure that Santa was wearing a baby front pack."

Her cheeks turn pink and her lips twitch up at the sides. "Santa is a multitasker."

I smile at her. "Thank you, Lovely. But you shouldn't have wasted any money on me."

"Can I tell you a secret?" She asks, her eyes sparkling.

"You can tell me anything," I answer her honestly.

She leans forward, eyes darting side to side. "I'm kinda rich."

I burst into laughter, knowing full well how much her and Blanche are worth. The sisters have requested an audience at Church in the new year. It seems they have an investment idea they want to run by the club.

I stare at her, looking pleased with herself, smiling down at her daughter snuggled against her chest. "Lovely?"

She looks up, settling her dark eyes on me. "Yes?"

"Merry Christmas."

* * *

Merry Christmas from the DRMC and Tombs family.

Thank you for reading!

Thank you so much for choosing to spend a little time with the characters I made up. What a wild ride!

If you want to know more about me or what I'm reading you can find me all over the place –

Follow me at my author page on Facebook

Friend me on Facebook

Join my group Cleo Browne's Babes

Follow me on Instagram

Keep your eyes peeled for upcoming books in the Devil's Rose MC Series!

About the author

Cleo Browne is the pen name of a neurospicy geeky girl from Aotearoa New Zealand. As a child, she realized very early on that she wasn't a people person, so she would spend all her time reading and writing her own stories. These stories usually ended with the line "and then they died." As an adult, she has gotten slightly more people-y (not much) and better at not killing all her characters off when she writes.

Cleo loves to write about women who don't need a man to do their dirty work and the hot alpha men who turn to mush when they watch their women handling business.

When she's not writing romance novels about strong, curvy women and the men who adore them, she hangs out at home with her hubby, her boys, and her ancient greyhound who likes to creepily watch her write.

Acknowledgements

First off, I'd like to thank all the wonderful readers who continue to keep taking chances on a kooky little woman from New Zealand. Without you all reading my books and loving my characters, I would have just faded away into obscurity, never to be seen or heard from again. So, thank you. I appreciate you all.

Second, I'd like to thank my author bestie and all round good biartch Shaye Torrel. Thank you so much for talking me off the cliff when I would freak out that I didn't know what I was doing. I still don't, but at least I'm not freaking out about it. I wouldn't be here without you, chick!

Thanks to my fantabulous alpha reader Sally Howells who encourages the crazy and the amazing Gabi Brockelsby who catches any untoward typos. You ladies rock!

And finally, thanks to my partner PN. Without his constant words of encouragement, "I really didn't think MC books were a thing," I would never have finished this book. Thanks also go to my boys. Ronnie, for being completely disinterested, and Louis for your two hour long phone calls that would eat into my writing time. Love you guys.

Cleo Browne Books

Rhodie – Devil's Rose MC Book One

August – A Tombs Security + Devil's Rose MC Crossover

Wire – Devil's Rose MC Book Two

Tav Devil's Rose MC Book Three

Devil's Rose MC Christmas Novella

Tank – Devil's Rose MC Book Four
In progress

www.ingramcontent.com/pod-product-compliance
Lightning Source LLC
Chambersburg PA
CBHW030414120726
47904CB00007B/2271